AN UNEXPECTED ATTRACTION

BOOK 3 OF THE *LOVE UNEXPECTED* SERIES

DELANEY DIAMOND

AN UNEXPECTED ATTRACTION
by Delaney Diamond

PROLOGUE

Twelve years ago...

"Life in Naples sounds idyllic, but aren't you a little biased?" Brenda teased.

"My biased opinion does not make what I say any less true," Jay informed her, keeping his eyes on the road.

Outside, rain banged against the windshield, dropping in pailfuls from the night sky. The wiper blades of the sedan launched back and forth across the glass at a frantic pace to keep up.

"I bet you didn't know Naples is the third largest city in Italy," he continued. A proud *napoletano*, he took every opportunity to speak of the historic city's finer attributes and promote the culture to anyone who listened. "You must visit one day. There is so much to see and do. Beautiful beaches along the coast. A lot of museums, all with important collections that tell the history of our country and the region. Then there is the Royal Palace of Naples—a must-see. And of course, the food in my home city is excellent."

"Of course," Brenda said, poker-faced.

He chuckled. She never missed an opportunity to needle him about his Italian pride. "Trust me, we have some of the best restaurants in the entire country. And if you want to eat real pizza, good pizza, *oh mio dio,*" he kissed his fingertips, "you will not find better than in Naples."

She sat angled toward him, listening attentively to his words. "You've convinced me, Jay. I will definitely visit one day."

"You should go when I'm at home. I will make sure you have a good experience." He glanced sideways at her to gauge her reaction to his suggestion.

She smiled a bit shyly, but certainly with pleasure. "Deal. I'll go when you're there and you can show me around."

Jay smiled, too, energized by her reaction, and began a descriptive conversation about his birthplace and family who still resided there.

All too soon, the car ride came to an end. The engaging talk had kept his mind from the sobering thought that they'd have to part when he arrived at her apartment. Heavy-hearted, he fell into a quiet funk, wishing he could extend their time alone together.

He pulled up outside the apartment building, but a couple of cars parked right in front of the door prevented him from pulling any closer.

"Darn," Brenda said, sighing. "Too bad we can't plough into their cars and make them move."

He heard the humor in the words but couldn't

respond to it. He didn't want her to go. "That wouldn't be very nice to hit their cars," he said.

She grinned at him. "I was kidding. You're such a good guy."

He stared straight ahead, jaw tightening. "I'm not a good guy." Good guys didn't contemplate ways to prolong their time with a woman they shouldn't want. Good guys didn't imagine that same woman naked.

"Why do you say you're not a good guy?" She sounded amused.

"Because I'm not."

An uncomfortable silence filled the car. There were things he wanted to say to her and internally debated if he should. Maybe he should tell her the truth about his feelings.

"It's really raining hard. I'll have to make a run for it," she said.

He should have popped the lock and let her out, but instead Jay pulled away from the building.

"What are you doing?" Brenda demanded.

He glided into a space farther away from the front door. It was Saturday night and only a few cars were in the parking lot because many of the student residents were out partying before they left for break.

He turned off the car and twisted to face her, summoning the courage to speak the words on his heart.

"What's going on?" she asked in a quiet voice. Lines of confusion marked her forehead.

"I think about you all the time," Jay said. A heavy weight lifted from his shoulders with that admission. He took her hand, and surprisingly, she let him. He stroked her slender fingers. Her skin felt like velvet. "I don't know what to do about the way I feel. It is like...like a torture I cannot be free from."

Her fingers curled against his palm. "Jenna's my friend."

He chose to ignore her words and tightened his hand around her fisted fingers, slowly prying them open, one by one and with very little resistance. He lowered his lips and planted a kiss in the middle of her palm. She didn't pull away, and her breathing pattern changed from normal to sporadic. Encouraged, he let his lips move in gentle strokes to the inside of her wrist.

He knew he was wrong. He knew he should stop. But all thoughts of stopping evaporated when she swayed toward him, lips parted, eyes pleading for more intimate contact.

After that, everything happened so fast. He pulled her across his lap so that she straddled him on the seat. The confines of the car made movement difficult, but he'd had to touch her.

Now, he had to taste her, too...

CHAPTER ONE

Present day

No reaction. Not laughter. Not even tears. His
death had devastated them all, and one day, Brenda
Morrison would look back on this night and
recognize it was the beginning of the end, the last
time the five of them came together as friends. Not
only because of his passing, but because of her own
personal evolution, and how her relationship with one
person in particular transformed against her better
judgment.

The somberness in her friends' faces was no doubt
reflected in her own. Charlie, the sixth member of
their rat pack crew, had been killed a mere month
before he was scheduled to tie the knot. Three thugs
had entered his home one afternoon and been
surprised when they encountered him. One of them
shot him in the back when he tried to escape. They'd
left her friend to die, bleeding out on the staircase in
his home. Had it not been for the very conspicuous

black BMW the teens had driven off in, back to their upper middle class neighborhood, the crime might have gone unsolved.

Brenda and her friends had attended the funeral and spent several hours with his family before coming to his favorite Italian restaurant for drinks—a casual dining establishment with two bars, an average menu but potent alcoholic beverages, and a dueling piano show that attracted customers from neighboring cities.

In her mind's eye she saw Charlie's dark brown skin and laughing eyes. He'd been a horrible procrastinator, but he'd never had a bad word to say about a single person. He didn't deserve such a vicious, untimely death. His sudden passing had left behind an empty hole in their hearts, a fiancée and, they'd learned today, an unborn child.

"He wouldn't want us to sit here like this," Sophie said. She sat beside Brenda with wild, curly hair and a host of colorful bangles and earrings, representative of her quirky style and personality. "He wouldn't want us to dwell on his death. He'd want us to talk about how he lived. Charlie loved having a good time. He'd want us to remember the good times and laugh."

She was right. Brenda opened her mouth to speak, to say something witty and funny about Charlie, but she couldn't find the words. Her heart heavy and filled with the pain of loss, she remained silent. So did everyone else.

"Come on, guys," Sophie pleaded. "Don't we owe it to Charlie to at least pay him his due?"

To Sophie's right sat Nick, who'd flown in from Europe. The wise-cracking member, his dark brown hair stood on end from constantly running his fingers through it. He'd been closer to Charlie than any of them, so understandably, he took his death the hardest. Brenda quietly kept an eye on how many glasses of Grey Goose vodka he consumed.

The silence remained—heavy, somber, until a smile lifted a corner of Nick's mouth.

"That son of a bitch owed me two thousand dollars for that quote, unquote, new-and-improved quattrocycle he created. No matter how many times I told him to forget about the money, he always insisted he'd pay me back." He leaned onto his forearms, gaze sweeping the table to encompass the group. "A couple of months ago he sent a spreadsheet with the total and the amount of interest that had accrued. He swore before the end of the year he would pay me back." He shook his head. "Crazy son of a bitch."

Charlie owned dozens of patents for mechanical creations no one had an interest in. Since college he had borrowed money from friends and worked on ideas he claimed would one day make him a millionaire. None of them had been successful, but he never quit trying.

"Guess you'll have to write off the debt after all," Jenna said. She sat across from Brenda with her chin resting in her hand. A few strands of lengthy blonde hair fell forward over her shoulder.

"Guess so," Nick agreed with a wry, mournful smile.

"He owed me ten thousand dollars." All eyes turned to Jay Santorini, Jenna's ex-husband. He sat to Jenna's left, subdued and slouched in a chair, tie undone. He'd placed his jacket over the back of the chair. Rolled up shirtsleeves revealed strong forearms sprinkled with a dusting of hair the same midnight shade as the curls on his head. Long fingers cradled a tumbler of Scotch, and every now and again he lifted the glass to take a minute sip.

"You gave him ten grand?" Nick asked. "What were you thinking?"

. "Multiple loans over the years." Jay shrugged. As the wealthiest member of their circle of friends, ten thousand probably hadn't put much of a dent in his finances. "I believed in him, and who could resist Charlie?"

They all nodded.

"Remember when he was looking into alternative fuels and went around to all those restaurants collecting oil at the end of the day?" Nick asked.

"Ohmigod," Sophie said, shaking her head. "Do you know that fool dragged me into that mess? He had me hitting up the wing joint and the soul food restaurant near my apartment, collecting oil for him."

"No, you didn't," Brenda said, laughing.

"Yes! Consider yourself lucky you lived in Chicago at the time, or he would have roped you in, too, I'm sure."

Jenna giggled, casting a sidelong glance at Jay. "Guess who put that *alternative* fuel in his Mercedes?"

"*No*," Sophie said, wide-eyed.

"In my defense, it was the older model." Jay's grey eyes lit with amusement. Brenda could still hear a little bit of his Italian accent, even though he'd lived in Georgia for years. He set his elbow on the table and pointed at no one in particular. "I'm telling you, I drove around for a whole week without having to buy gas. Charlie was onto something."

They all fell out laughing, and that was the beginning of the Charlie stories.

Jay ordered appetizers, and before long plenty of alcoholic beverages and mediocre Italian food accompanied the reminiscing. Spirits lifted, they became the most raucous table in the restaurant, but they ignored the dirty looks from the other patrons. Tonight was about Charlie and celebrating his life.

Sometime later, Jenna covered a wide yawn with her hand. "I'd better get going," she said.

Nick frowned and looked at his watch. "It's early—only eight thirty."

"By the time I get back to the hotel and settle down for the night, it'll be late. My flight leaves in the morning, and I need to check on the boys before I go to bed." Jenna and Jay had two boys, ten-year-old fraternal twins. "Mind walking me out?" she asked Jay in a low voice.

She placed a hand on his hair-sprinkled forearm to get his attention. Brenda looked away from the sight of them touching, settling her attention on the dueling pianists prepping the stage for their act.

She didn't hear Jay's response, but he and Jenna stood at the same time, prompting a round of goodbyes and hugs. Jay walked her out while the rest of them remained at the table. At least fifteen minutes passed before he came back, and when he did, his expression was grim. Brenda briefly wondered what had happened but didn't dare ask. She steered clear of anything involving Jay and Jenna.

The dueling pianists started their set, part musical and part comedic show. Both musicians sang loud and strong, and at one point one of them played with his toes. Not to be outdone, the other countered by climbing on top of the piano, hanging over the edge, and tapping out his song on the keys, all while upside down and backwards.

Brenda hopped up from the table. "Let's dance," she said. There wasn't a dance floor, but she dragged Sophie from the chair to the front of the stage. Sophie was her partner in crime and could always be counted on to go along with a wild idea, not to mention she came up with many of her own.

Encouraged by whistles and whooping from Jay, Nick, and a table of young professionals, she and Sophie worked up a sweat doing the bump, the mashed potato, and the twist to doo-wop music from the 1960's. They sang along with the musicians and danced away the pain of loss. When a couple of older men joined them in front of the stage, even more patrons cheered and clapped, turning the quartet into impromptu stars of the restaurant.

Finally, the pianists took a break, and the dancing ended.

"We had a little help with the set tonight," the pianist on the left said into the microphone. "Another round of applause for these lovely ladies and their very lucky partners."

Most of the patrons rose to their feet and applauded. Sophie curtsied, Brenda bowed with a flourish, and their dance partners inclined their heads.

Brenda's partner placed a hand on her shoulder. "Thank you for the dance. I'm pretty sure I broke something, but it was worth it to have a dance with a lovely young woman like you." He winked and followed his friend to their table.

"Did you hear him?" she asked Sophie.

"I did. Consider yourself lucky. The guy I danced

with tried to get my phone number. He's old enough to be my father!"

Out of breath and laughing hysterically, they stumbled back to their table and fell into the chairs.

They all lingered over drinks and picked at the remains of food on their plates, loathed to go their separate ways because times like these—when they could be together and have fun away from the grind of daily life—had become rare over the years.

Jay ordered another round of drinks, and when everyone had taken sips and quiet descended on the table, he held up his glass. "To living life to the fullest, with no regrets. And to Charlie, for teaching us how to live. Cheers."

"To Charlie," the others echoed, and they clinked their glasses together in the middle of the table.

Under the weight of memories and nostalgia, Brenda stood, swaying a little with the half empty glass of Long Island Iced Tea in her hand.

"Careful now," Jay teased.

She placed a hand on her hip. "I'm always careful," she said tartly.

His mouth smiled, but those eyes of his watched her closely. That assessing expression appeared every so often and always gave her pause. What was he thinking when he looked at her that way?

"Speech, speech, speech," Nick and Sophie chorused.

She waved them into silence and took a deep breath. "I feel as if I've known you guys all my life. We've been through a lot together, and if I never told you before, I hope you know how important you are to me. I'm loving this new chapter in my life." She'd been the east coast editor of *The Entertainment Report*, headquartered in Los Angeles, for a little over six months. She had the ability to craft her edition of the magazine in almost any way she wanted, an editor's dream. "I love my new job and the opportunities it's presented. I'm so glad I have good friends like you Sophie, Nick…" Her throat tightened with sentimentality as her gaze landed on each of them. When it moved to Jay, she saw an unidentifiable emotion flicker in the depths of his eyes, one that momentarily stole her breath and sent her heart tripping over itself. "And Jay." She swallowed and looked away from him or she'd never be able to finish. Her heart beat as fast as when she'd danced in front of the stage. Perhaps she'd had way more to drink than she realized. "Words can't express how much you all mean to me."

"Awww," Sophie said.

Brenda placed a finger over her lips. "Shhh. This is my moment." There were soft chuckles around the table. "Seriously, though, here's to good friends. I love you all!"

"Here, here!" her friends yelled.

They clinked their glasses together again, and she took a deep swallow from hers.

"Now sit your butt down." Sophie pulled her back onto the seat and into a hug. "Love you, too," she whispered. Charlie's death had made the word *love* flow freely all day long.

The waitress arrived at the table, a pretty redhead named Gina. "Can I get you anything else?" she asked. Her gaze encompassed the entire group before settling on Jay.

"Unless you're going to give me your number, I'm fine," he said with a playful grin. Often the charmer and flirt, his behavior came as no surprise.

Gina blushed. "Would any of you like more to drink? More to eat?"

It was obvious she was interested. She didn't take her eyes off of him. With his dark Italian looks and short beard, he exuded masculinity. He could have her in the cooler in the back if he tried hard enough. Brenda stared down into her almost empty glass.

"Just the check," Jay said. "I'm picking up the tab for this bunch of hooligans. Please thank the management for not kicking us out."

"Awww, isn't he generous?" Nick hooked his arm around Jay's neck.

"I'll pay for everybody but this guy," Jay added, pointing at his friend with his thumb.

Sophie tossed her cloth napkin across the table and it landed on his empty plate. "You're terrible," she said. Her eyes flirted with him, and Jay grinned but didn't offer further encouragement.

Sophie didn't lack male attention, but she remained in an on-again-off-again relationship with a man who was no good for her, which tended to limit her dating options. Brenda had never suspected Sophie might be interested in Jay, but the moment that passed between them suggested otherwise. Unease lodged in her chest and warmed the spot right beneath her sternum, making her toss back the watery remnants of the Long Island Iced Tea.

Gina bussed the table and Jay took the black leather checkbook she handed him. He looked inside and immediately glanced up in Gina's direction, but she had already walked away with their empty plates. A slow, stealthy smile spread across his face. He looked very much like someone who'd received exactly what he wanted. No doubt Gina had supplied her phone number. Surprise, surprise.

Jay's gaze collided with Brenda's and she froze. She hadn't meant to stare, but that's exactly what she'd done and quickly looked away, albeit too late.

She'd grown accustomed to seeing women react to Jay. They were often drawn to him.

He wasn't overly tall, topping out a little over six feet, but when he entered a room he called attention to himself *without* calling attention to himself. He really didn't *do* anything, except be...Jay. Casually sexy in the way that some men are. Under the right circumstances his smile turned impish, which when paired with his other physical attributes, made him spectacular to look at. Most women could easily be seduced by the slightest bit of interest from a man like him.

Most.

If things were different...

Brenda dismissed her musing as that of someone who'd clearly had too much to drink. She shouldn't hypothesize about what could have been. No point in having her thoughts go in that direction.

Years ago that bridge had been crossed, burned, and charred to a brittle crisp.

Chapter Two

Jay stepped onto the sidewalk with Nick and the women, pulling his jacket closed to protect against the cool, early April air. Cars drove by on the street, and there was a little bit of foot traffic because of the high-end shopping center where they had eaten.

"I'm not looking forward to tomorrow," Nick said, shoving his fingers through his too-long hair. "My flight leaves at six in the morning." He groaned.

As the import director of a consumer food products company, he spent a lot of time overseas. He'd come back for a couple of days because of Charlie's funeral but wouldn't be back again until July.

Brenda stifled a yawn and swayed. Her shoulder bumped Jay. Reflexively, he caught her around the waist with a steadying arm. "You okay?" he asked.

His gaze slid over her upturned face, taking in the darkness of her skin—deep brown, like his favorite amaretto. The black wrap dress molded to her figure, and he felt her softness under the thin layer of fabric. She wore her hair cut short in a tapered pixie that flattered her oval face, with strands winging over her right eye and touching her eyelash.

She grinned and eased from his arm. "I'm tired and ready for bed." She yawned again, looking rather sleepy, eyes struggling to stay open. She brushed the bangs of her hair out of her face. "Either that or I'm turning into a lightweight. I can't believe I let you three force me to drink so much."

Sophie snorted.

"Forced you?" Nick said, pretending to be insulted. "We couldn't stop you if we tried."

"We couldn't stop the dancing, either," Jay said.

"I'm ignoring you. All of you." Brenda pointed at each of them.

Jay pulled out his phone and checked the time. They had been one of Gina's last tables, and she would be getting off soon. He'd learned her schedule after she left her number in the checkbook. He'd made a trek to the restroom and stopped her on his way there.

"Do you have somewhere to go?" Brenda asked, one eyebrow raised.

"Jay's always got somewhere to go and some*one* to do," Nick said.

Oh boy. Now Nick would start his routine where he teased Jay mercilessly about his sexual exploits, and Sophie and Brenda would jump right in.

"Nothing's changed, has it?" Brenda eyed him with part amusement and something else. Disapproval, maybe?

"Jacopo Santorini, the Italian Stallion," Nick said. He neighed like a horse.

"That's enough," Jay said. When he'd first heard the name, he hadn't known whether to be flattered or insulted. He happened to enjoy women and enjoyed sex. Lucky for him, he found them both in abundance.

"Well, don't let us keep you," Sophie chimed in. "Go do your thing—or that person."

Jay pointed at Nick. "See what you've started?"

They all laughed at his expense, and right then the taxi Brenda had called pulled up at the curb. Brenda pouted, an attempt at playful petulance, but with her full, lush mouth, she came across as tempting and provocative. Jay's eyes lingered on her lips far longer than they should have, and his breathing suspended, as if someone had cut off his oxygen.

Brenda sighed. "This is it, gentlemen. We need to do a better job of keeping in touch."

Did she mean it, or was that simply the polite thing to say?

She walked over to Nick and gave him a long hug. "Bye-bye," she said softly. "Have a safe trip, and tell your mother hello for me." When he went back to Europe, Nick planned to stop off in Greece first, where his extended family lived.

"I will. She always asks about you." Nick squeezed her tight and briefly pressed his face into her neck. Feeling as if he was intruding on a private moment, Jay looked away. He and Sophie exchanged hugs then stood silently as Brenda and Nick spoke softly, their heads close together.

Then Brenda walked over to give Jay a hug, too. She smelled sweet and flowery, but he couldn't place the fragrance. "It was good to see you," she whispered. Again he wondered if she meant it. She'd lived in Atlanta for six months, but neither of them had made an effort to get together.

He smiled and wrapped his arms around her waist, pulling her close enough to feel the full weight of her soft breasts and have her stiffen against him. The temptation to continue holding her was strong. He yearned to also bury his face in her neck, as Nick had done. But their hug didn't last nearly as long as the one she gave their friend. They never did. Almost immediately she pulled back, and his hand clenched at the loss of contact.

"It was good to see you, too. Get some sleep, lightweight," he teased, tweaking the tip of her nose.

Brenda wrinkled it at him. "I will," she sang as she sashayed to the waiting taxi. Sophie followed behind. From the backseat, they both waved and blew kisses out the window. He and Nick watched until the car disappeared.

His friend sighed deeply. "She's great, isn't she?" A wistful note filled his voice.

"Which one?" Jay asked, though he really knew.

"Brenda, of course."

Of course.

Brenda attracted people no matter where she went. She was quite a character, with a cute little laugh that came easily and often, and was the kind of person who never met a stranger. One of those people who struck up conversations in grocery store lines and made lifelong friends as a result.

"Yeah, she's great," he agreed, keeping his tone neutral. Like Nick, he stared down the street where the cab had disappeared, a pain in his jaw from clenching his teeth so hard.

****

The taxicab rolled with a mild flow of traffic, the soothing voice of a talk radio host coming through the speakers. Brenda rested her head against the seat and yawned. She shouldn't have drunk so much. She'd probably have a terrible headache tomorrow.

"I can't believe how you have Nick eating out of your hand," Sophie said from beside her.

They were on the way to Brenda's house, where Sophie had left her jeep. She was spending the night instead of taking the long drive back to her apartment. As a flight attendant, she did like many airline employees and lived south of the city for an easy commute to the airport.

"You're making this into a bigger deal than it is. He's just being nice." She shouldn't have told her what Nick whispered out on the sidewalk.

"Being nice?" She couldn't see Sophie's face clearly in the dark vehicle, but she didn't have to. The skepticism came through loud and clear. "He invited you to go to Europe, all expenses paid, and he didn't offer the same to me or Jay. I'm pretty sure he's trying to get in your panties."

Brenda didn't respond to Sophie's assertion because, in all honesty, she had her doubts about Nick's motives. His invitation had taken her by surprise.

Sophie yawned. "I'm exhausted."

"Me, too."

Silence.

"Jay's so hot," Sophie said. "But he's not the least bit interested in me."

Brenda lifted her head. "How could you even think about getting involved with Jay when…?"

"When what? Because of Jenna?" Sophie waved her hand dismissively. "Please, those two have been divorced for ten years, and they've both been involved with other people since then."

"Other people, but not one of us," Brenda said pointedly.

"Um, again, they're divorced, and she's more your friend than mine, if we're honest."

"I cannot believe you," Brenda said.

"What? So she gets to call dibs on his penis for the rest of his life? Pfft. Please. There are people who give up their families because of love."

"Are you saying you're in love with him?" The question came out as a high-pitched squeal and her heart quivered, a rapid movement that left her a little breathless.

"Heck no! But I'd give up her friendship in a second for Jay."

Brenda gaped at Sophie. "Remind me never to let you near my future husband."

"I would never sleep with your husband, and besides, you're the best of my besties. That's a no-no, but if after you're done with him and it's true love…" She shrugged as she let the words trail off.

"Wow." Brenda let out a short laugh and shook her head.

"You can have your goody-two-shoes crap. I'd rather have true love."

"It's not crap. There are just things you don't do, that's all."

"And this has nothing to do with your mommy issues," Sophie said dryly.

Brenda ignored her.

She and her mother had an odd relationship, but she didn't have mommy issues. Her mother refused to grow up, and Brenda had always been the adult in their mother-daughter relationship. She'd always been responsible, prone to make the right decisions with her head, while her mother tended to go with her heart and hormones.

"But seriously, why do you think Jay's never shown any interest in me?" Sophie asked. "I dropped a few hints tonight, but he didn't appear to be the least bit interested."

"Probably because you spent so much time talking about Keith, like you always do," Brenda said.

Sophie swung her head in Brenda's direction. "Did I talk about him a lot?"

"He kept coming up."

"Ugh. Oh well. That waitress is probably under Jay as we speak."

"Probably." Brenda folded her arms, eyes trained on the passing cars and the bright lights of the shopping center they'd stopped in front of, wishing away the prickle of pain in her chest.

After the driver pulled off, Sophie turned her head in Brenda's direction. "Hey, are you okay? You seem off."

"I'm tired," Brenda replied. It wasn't entirely untrue. Even though it was Saturday, she'd gone into work for a few hours before swinging back home to meet Sophie and go to the funeral. Add to that the long day, the dancing, and the drinking, she looked forward to sliding under the sheets and sleeping late tomorrow.

Sophie rested her head against the seat of the cab and closed her eyes. "I've always wondered what happened, you know, between Jay and Jenna. They were together for a couple of years, got married, but the marriage didn't even last two years. Why? I mean, look at him. I would have tried to work that out, whatever the problem was."

"Jenna said irreconcilable differences caused the divorce." Brenda didn't know the whole story, but Jenna had mentioned something vague about them realizing too late that they'd made a mistake. She'd never heard Jay's side. She'd never asked.

Sophie tilted her head in Brenda's direction. "Maybe it wasn't a love match. She was pregnant when they got married."

Brenda shrugged. "I don't know. Who knows why people get married or divorced?"

"People get married because they're in love."

"Not always. People marry for all kinds of reasons."

"True." Sophie closed her eyes again. "I know I made those comments about Jay, but it's sad their marriage didn't last. I thought for sure they were so in love. I knew, of all our friends who'd married young, their marriage would last. But it was the shortest lived. The boys turned out great, but it's too bad things didn't work out between them."

Brenda looked out the window again. They'd rolled to a stop at another red light. On the sidewalk, a couple speed-walked arm-in-arm.

"Yeah. Too bad things didn't work out," she said quietly.

CHAPTER THREE

Brenda slammed the car door and ran up the stone steps to the porch. She had about an hour to shower, change, drive to Sweet Treats Bakery, and get to her board meeting at the Fulton County Performing Arts & Community Center. She served on the fundraising committee of the center, which brought diverse programming to the area and boasted a state-of-the-art theater with the latest in digital and audio equipment. She probably couldn't make the meeting on time, but was determined to try.

Her home was the first floor apartment of a 1920's duplex in Candler Park. It was a long drive to and from her job in Alpharetta, but she'd immediately fallen in love with the place because of its charming façade and the way light came into the house. An added bonus was its proximity to the park, which served as a venue for festivals throughout the year, and the restaurants and shops within walking distance.

Inside, she hung her keys on the key rack and

walked down the hallway to one of the two bedrooms. Although the house had been renovated five years ago, the owner had maintained the character of the original construction with simple touches like refurbishing the cabinets and repairing the solid wood floors.

She tossed her purse on the queen size bed, the only new furniture in the entire apartment. It was Victorian in design, with an antique bronze headboard and footboard. Every other piece of furniture she owned had been purchased secondhand, including the distressed oak dresser.

Making good time, Brenda had changed and was in the process of locking up when she saw her neighbor and landlord from upstairs, Mrs. Chen, carrying two bags filled with groceries. She was an elderly white woman with a twinkle in her blue eyes that suggested despite the bent shoulders and slow walk, her energy and spirit remained intact. She always had a friendly greeting whenever they ran into each other, so Brenda didn't hesitate to approach her.

"Need help with those?" she asked, pointing to the two totes, one in each of Mrs. Chen's hands.

"You don't mind?" Brenda had assisted her before, but she always asked.

"Not at all." She was short on time but couldn't allow her neighbor to lug those bags up the stairs by herself.

"I appreciate it so much." Her voice sounded weary. Brenda took the bags and followed her up the stairs to the second floor. They progressed slowly, Mrs. Chen holding the handrail and taking her time with unhurried, measured steps.

Inside the apartment, Brenda set the totes on the

kitchen counter. "There you go. Anything else I can help you with?"

"Aren't you a kind-hearted soul." Mrs. Chen held up a finger. "Wait one minute." She shuffled over to an old-fashioned ceramic cookie jar and pulled off the lid. But when she looked inside the container, her expression changed from smiling to disappointment. "I was going to give you some of my snickerdoodle cookies. I baked a whole batch a few days ago, but my grandson came by. He must have eaten them all."

"That's okay. I'm on my way to the bakery before my meeting tonight. I bring them dessert to make the meeting a little more pleasant."

"I'll make some more very soon," Mrs. Chen promised, "and bring them down to you."

"It's okay, really," Brenda said, wanting to put the older woman's mind at ease.

"No, I insist." Mrs. Chen walked Brenda to the front door.

When she stepped outside, Brenda turned to the older woman. "I have a question to ask you."

"Go right ahead."

"Why do you live on the second floor? Why not take the first floor apartment?" She'd wondered this from the beginning, ever since the first time she'd seen Mrs. Chen trudge up the stairs.

The corners of her landlord's mouth tilted up into a wistful, almost pained expression. "My husband and I lived in this apartment for thirty-five years." She leaned against the door, as if the weight of the memories had tipped her off balance. "It wasn't love at first sight. He was a small man and not my usual type. I wasn't his, either." She laughed softly, her features brightening so much her wrinkles seemed to vanish. "But our relationship evolved—against the wishes of our families. Back then, things were very much different for people who didn't...look the same." Her voice lowered, her eyes passing a message. "It was us against the world, and together we were unstoppable, could do anything. We bought this house, fixed it, and rented out the downstairs. We raised our daughter and our son here. We struggled, we laughed, we made a lot of memories. Yes, it would be easier for me to move downstairs, but then I'd have to say goodbye. I'm not ready to say goodbye to Huan yet."

Tears sprang to Brenda's eyes. How beautiful it must be to find a love like that. A love worth sacrificing for and worth whatever you'd have to give up.

"Thank you for sharing that story." She reached for Mrs. Chen's wrinkled hand, so fragile she felt the brittle bones beneath her delicate skin. "Whenever you need my help, promise me you'll knock on my door. Don't hesitate."

Mrs. Chen squeezed Brenda's fingers. "You're such a sweetheart. You don't need to be bothered by a crazy old woman." She chuckled. "Now I have a question for you. Are you seeing anyone?" Her eyes sparkled with mischief.

"Oh no, don't you dare." Brenda waved her hands vigorously. "I get enough of everyone playing matchmaker."

Since returning to Atlanta, her friends Jenna and Sophie, even an employee had tried to set her up. With her new job at the magazine, she simply hadn't had time to get out and meet anyone. She aimed to remedy the situation soon now that she'd settled into the editor position.

"Hmm...How old are you? Thirty-one, thirty-two?"

"Good guess, I'm thirty-two, but—"

"I know a couple of good young men your age. Let me know if you're interested and I'll arrange for you to meet one or two of them."

That was definitely Brenda's cue to leave tout de suite before Mrs. Chen married her off to one of those 'good young men.'

"I will keep that in mind, but I have to run so I'm not late for my meeting."

She hurried down the stairs and away from her landlord's good intentions.

****

If it weren't for the fact that Sweet Treats Bakery made the best cannoli outside of his dearly departed *nonna*, Jay wouldn't even bother coming to the popular bakery. Calling ahead and placing an order as he'd done in the past would have been wise, but the urge to come didn't hit until he was nearby.

Running the largest advertising firm in the southeast sometimes meant long days, but seldom did he have to work as hard as he had over the past couple of months to convince a client to hire his firm. After a long, drawn out meeting this afternoon, the client—a flamboyant former rapper by the name of DJ Terror, intent on rebranding his image—finally signed with Omega Advertising. Jay felt like he had earned this treat.

He exited his Mercedes SUV, a sleek, bullet gray machine purchased a year ago. His devotion to the brand had started during childhood. His grandfather, the most influential male figure in his life after his parents divorced and his father moved to the States, only bought Mercedes.

"Good, dependable car," he would say, and slap his hand on the roof to emphasize the point.

An ache filled Jay's chest. To this day, he still missed his grandfather, who'd raised him to be a man of upstanding moral character. Nothing like the so-called father who'd given Jay five, *or more*, half-siblings scattered around the globe.

Jay trekked across the parking lot, and lo and behold spotted Brenda entering the bakery ahead of him. He hadn't seen her since the funeral three weeks ago. The sight of her lifted his spirits and lightened his steps. Upon entering the store, crammed with customers getting their end-of-the-day fix, the scent of fresh baked breads, cakes, and pies hit his nose and made his mouth water.

Brenda stood in one of the three lines, staring up at the menu board.

He strolled up behind her, his olfactory sense immediately immersed in a combined cloud of perfume and her own unique fragrance. The combination was more enticing than the baked goods. He bent close to her ear. "I'm not surprised."

Brenda jumped and swung around to face him, covering her heart with her hand. "You scared me." She laughed nervously and then tilted her head at him, a soft smile on her face. "What's that supposed to mean, anyway?"

Damn, she looked great, but that wasn't unusual. Her skin glowed and those big, expressive brown eyes sparkled with a teasing light. Was it any wonder his spirits lifted as soon as he saw her?

"You, *signorina*, have an uncanny ability for finding

the best bakeries."

She laughed, a husky sound filled with warmth and sensuality that sent shivers down his spine.

Calm down, Jacopo.

"I'm here to pick up snacks for a meeting I have later, but you're one to talk. Let me guess." She screwed up her face into a thoughtful frown and looked up at him from behind a veil of thick lashes. "The cannolis must be exceptional here."

"Cannoli—no "s" at the end," he corrected. "It's already plural."

"You mean I've been saying it wrong all these years?" Her eyes widened in mock distress.

"Afraid so," he said with the appropriate amount of gravity in his voice. "And that completes today's lesson in *italiano*."

She giggled, a lighter sound this time that still generated tiny tremors on his skin.

"But you're right, they do have really good cannoli here," Jay confessed.

"Uh-huh, I knew it!" She wagged a finger at him. "I know your M.O., too, mister. You're craving comfort food and came to where you knew you'd get it. You really need to learn self-control."

She looked mighty pleased with herself that she'd called him out. Eyes bright, full lips curved up. He had brought that animated expression to her face.

"I don't seem to have any self-control when it comes to certain things," he said in a low voice.

The words had slipped out. In response, her smile dimmed with uncertainty for a nanosecond.

The line moved forward and they moved with it.

Jay scanned the menu board. Different colored chalk scrawled across the blackboard announced a fifty-percent off sale on focaccia bread. He'd buy a couple of loaves and place one in the freezer for later.

"Did you finally unpack?" he asked.

The day of Charlie's funeral, Brenda had confessed that after a year, she still had unpacked boxes lying around.

"Finally. Charlie's death made me think about all the things I'd left undone that needed to be completed. No more putting off until tomorrow what could be done today."

He'd had similar thoughts. Charlie had postponed marrying his high school sweetheart for years, too focused on his job and the projects he'd worked on. Only when she'd threatened to finally leave him did he give in to the pressure of setting a date. They'd planned to have a civil ceremony at the courthouse, but all too soon he was gone.

Brenda turned halfway toward him. "How about you? How's the house coming?"

"They estimate it'll be completed by the fall."

Having lived close to the city for years, Jay had decided to build a five-bedroom home with a full basement in Alpharetta, close to good schools and right in the middle of suburban life. The move had been precipitated by the fact that his boys were moving from Bradenton, Florida to live with him in Atlanta next year. They'd be at the age when he felt they needed more of a male influence as they grew into young men. He couldn't wait to play a more active role in their lives.

"My office is in Alpharetta," Brenda said.

"Right off the parkway, right?"

She nodded. "I'm so happy for you. So it'll be you and the boys in a bachelor pad, huh? Watch out,

Atlanta."

He chuckled. "It won't be that bad."

To be honest, he hadn't thought the move would ever happen. When he'd first broached the topic to Jenna a few years ago, she'd expressed reservations. Eventually she'd come around to his way of thinking, but in typical fashion, she'd backpedaled when he'd walked her out to the car at the Italian restaurant. She'd claimed she couldn't let her "babies" go. An argument had ensued, but Jay had been adamant the boys were coming to live with him. They were excited, he was excited. End of story.

"Once the house is completed, I promised they could pick their own bedroom colors and decorate any way they want—within reason, of course."

"Of course. There always has to be a caveat when you make an offer to kids."

"Always." The line moved again and they shuffled forward. "So what meeting do you have this afternoon?"

"I'm on the board of the Fulton County Performing Arts & Community Center. We have a big fundraiser coming up in the fall, and there's a board meeting tonight. Pray for me that I don't strangle anyone."

"I promise to say three Hail Marys." He did the sign of the cross.

"Thank you," Brenda said, with exaggerated gratitude. She swept hair higher on her forehead, and he had a vague recollection of filtering the soft strands through his fingers. "I'm tired of hearing excuses for why the other committee members haven't done their part. I've done mine. Through my media contacts I'm able to get the word out, using bloggers and other channels, but my other task is to secure the celebrity appearances. Tyler Perry has already committed and even offered a five-figure donation. God bless him. The man is generous to a fault. The MC has a popular morning show, and I'm waiting to hear from an Academy Award winning actress—who shall remain nameless because I don't want to jinx it."

The line moved forward and they edged forward, too.

Jay thought for a moment. An idea formulated in his head. "You need anyone else? I signed a new client today and this fundraiser sounds like the kind of thing he's expressed interest in doing to revamp his image."

Her brow furrowed with tiny little creases. "Who did you have in mind?"

"Have you heard of DJ Terror?"

"The rapper? Of course." He had her attention. "But I thought you only worked with businesses."

"DJ Terror—or rather, Vince Combes—is a business," Jay explained. "During his years as a rap artist he invested well and if he never wanted to work again now that he's retired, he doesn't have to. His empire includes stakes in real estate and restaurants, and he's a silent partner in a number of other ventures. But he's still young—only thirty-five—and wants to stay busy. He's worked on his paintings—"

"Did you say *paintings*?"

The incredulous expression on her face made him laugh. "Yes. He's painted abstracts for years but is only now willing to share his art with the world. He works in oils and plans to unveil his best pieces in a small exhibition this summer. He'll do at least one performance painting at the venue, which means while he paints, music plays and influences the design of the final product. Interested?"

"Absolutely. It would be great for us to get someone so well known. Even better if he'd do a performance painting at the center." Her eyes lit up with the possibilities. "You know, we could do a couple of features on him for the magazine, leading up to the event. It could help establish his new image. What do you think?"

"I think it's a great idea. I'll talk to the head of my creative services department and get back to you."

Free publicity was better than any ad Omega Advertising could purchase. Creative services would jump at the chance to do the features. The team just had to decide on the best strategy for incorporating them into the overall plan.

"Excellent." She rubbed her hands together and turned back around. Knowing Brenda, her mind was probably spinning angles for the articles already.

His eyes settled on her exposed neck, and he had a sudden urge to touch her skin, to hear her softly inhale as he traced a hand down her spine. His gaze continued a downward slide over her shoulders and the silver cowl-neck blouse that hugged her body without being too revealing. Lower still, he took stock of the black, wide-legged pants and stopped. His body tensed, and he tore his eyes away from her hips and ass before the vulgar thoughts that had flashed through his mind took such control they manifested outwardly and he embarrassed himself in the line.

When he'd calmed down enough to speak again, he said, "You know how we were talking about getting together more often? You and Sophie should come to game night at my house. It's a lot of fun. Adult fun."

"Oh?" She sounded interested, but as she dug in her purse, he only saw her profile and couldn't tell if she really was or not. "When's the next one?"

"In a couple of weeks."

She raised her eyes to his. "Do we have to bring anything?"

"Only if you want to, but I have plenty of food and beverages, so it's not necessary."

She pulled out her wallet while he waited for a response. What was going through that head of hers?

"So what do you think?" he pressed. "Do you think you'll come?"

"I might be able to swing that," she said over her shoulder.

"Next!" The cashier's sharp cry broke into their conversation. No one else stood in front of Brenda, and they'd both been distracted enough to hold up the line.

She hurried forward and made her purchase. Afterward, she waited for him near the door, out of the flow of traffic. Once he had his box of cannoli, Jay joined her and they strolled out to the parking lot. As they walked, he gave her the details of game night, including the time and his address, since she'd never been to his house.

They ended their walk at her gold Jetta.

"So you're definitely coming?" he asked.

"Yes, Jay, I'll be there." She rolled her eyes. "With bells on. Happy?"

"Definitely wear the bells."

He winked at her and she gave him one of her Brenda grins—one that lit up her face and made him wish their situation was different. That there wasn't the occasional awkwardness between them and he could, without hesitation or second thought, pull her into his arms and not feel her stiffen.

He waited until her car started before he walked away toward his vehicle. As she cruised by, she honked and waved.

Jay waved back and was at his car, staring at his smiling face reflected in the driver side window, when he realized he'd actually been smiling almost the entire time he talked to Brenda. Nothing unusual about that at all. Her presence always brightened his day.

****

Brenda had wanted to decline Jay's invitation. For the most part she'd managed to steer clear of him since she moved back to Atlanta, but a visit to his house wouldn't be unpleasant if Sophie was there, and she did want to meet new people. She needed to get out more. Most of the past six months had been spent working hard at *The Entertainment Report*, so most every new person she met was in the entertainment industry. She could slow down now, and game night sounded like fun.

She was at the light and turning out of the parking lot when she caught her reflection in the rear view mirror. Her eyes were bright and she grinned like a fool, a complete one-eighty from her less than enthusiastic attitude about the board meeting tonight.

All because of Jay. He'd brightened her day.

CHAPTER FOUR

Sophie bailed on Brenda at the last minute. So last minute, in fact, Brenda was already en route to Jay's house when her friend called.

"I'm really sorry, but Keith wants me to go to this concert with him, and I'd feel terrible if I don't go and he spent all that money on a ticket."

"It's not your fault. He waited until the last minute to tell you." After the person he really wanted to take had canceled, no doubt.

But Brenda kept that comment to herself. No point in wasting her breath on another anti-Keith tirade. Sophie never listened. Brenda sometimes wondered if Keith had cast a spell on her friend. Her judgment where he was concerned could be considered questionable at best.

Brenda parked on the street and took a deep breath. She exited the car, holding a box of miniature cupcakes. Instead of a swanky bachelor pad in the middle of the city, Jay lived in a four-bedroom, three bath craftsman in Grant Park, one of the oldest neighborhoods in the Atlanta area. This location made sense considering its proximity to the Omega Advertising offices in the city, and that the neighborhood was family-friendly—perfect for when his sons visited.

From the street, she saw people milling around inside, and music and conversation spilled from the open windows. After climbing the stairs from street level, Brenda walked across the lawn and up the front steps of the porch. She lifted her hand to knock on the door, but it swung in and a woman with curly raven hair stood in the doorway. Her scarlet top and tan slacks made Brenda feel underdressed in plaid capri pants and a black cotton shirt.

"Hello and welcome," the brunette said. Her voice was surprisingly loud and she spoke with flawless diction. "I'm Dr. Helen Stafford." She presented her hand.

The formal introduction took Brenda by surprise, but she quickly recovered and extended her hand and a smile to the other woman. If she had a Ph.D., she might be inclined to tell everyone, too.

"Brenda Morrison."

After two solid pumps, the handshake was over.

"Jay is in the kitchen uncorking more wine," Helen said. She took the box of cupcakes. The room they entered was long and wide, taking up the entire front of the house. Large, comfy-looking furniture filled the room. "Let me introduce you to everyone." She turned to the room and yelled, "Everyone, this is Brenda Morrison. Make her feel welcome."

The fifteen or so men and women turned in their direction and said in unison, "Hi, Brenda!" Several of them waved.

She laughed and waved back, instantly glad she had come.

Helen guided her toward the kitchen, past the four people seated near the unlit fireplace who were slowly, meticulously, building a tower with Jenga blocks. A good-looking black man, standing and eating with another man who looked Hispanic, followed her with his eyes and gave a head nod as she walked by. Two other men sat in leather chairs in a corner, gesticulating wildly. She heard snatches of their conversation. They were debating the new gun law that had recently passed in the state legislature. Other people were scattered around the large room, including four seated on folding chairs at a collapsible table playing Uno.

Brenda entered the kitchen behind Helen, and not surprisingly, it was a flashy showpiece with cherry wood cabinets and stainless steel appliances. She didn't expect anything less than the best from Jay. Warming trays filled with delicious-smelling food sat on the granite countertops. He stood with his back to them, pouring a bottle of red wine into a glass decanter to breathe.

"Another guest has arrived," Helen announced.

Jay lifted his gaze when she came into his line of vision. He smiled, his grey eyes filled with genuine pleasure that she had come, and a tingle of awareness manifested in Brenda's midsection.

He looked relaxed and comfortable in black jeans that fit but weren't tight, and offered a hint at the muscular thighs underneath. A black long-sleeved Henley grasped his firm torso and pulled a little around the biceps. His curly hair, lush and glossy under the overhead lights, dipped onto his forehead and presented an attractive contrast against his creamy, olive-toned skin.

Alarm bells went off in her head. This was Jay, not a random man with rugged good looks and a cleft in his chin so deep she could probably sink her finger in up to the knuckle. Jay, her friend. Jay, who remained untouchable.

"Welcome," he said. "From what I heard, you've already met everyone." An eyebrow arched in inquiry.

"You could say that."

Helen retrieved a platter from the cupboard and proceeded to place the cupcakes on it. She moved around the space like someone very familiar with her surroundings. She must be Jay's latest girlfriend.

"Where's Sophie?" Jay asked. He worked on opening another bottle of red wine.

"She had to cancel." Brenda shrugged.

"Keith?"

"Of course."

He shook his head and poured some wine. Deep red climbed the inside of the glass. He passed it to her. "Drink up. There's plenty more where this came from."

The rest of the night was spent in entertaining conversations, from the best place to buy the freshest fruits and vegetables, to spirited debates about politics and the latest hot topics in the news. When the other guests learned Brenda was an entertainment editor, she became the center of attention. They grilled her about her experiences with the stars, but she gave diplomatic answers in reply to questions about celebrities behaving badly.

"Come on," Tomas said.

He was a big, brawny Cuban whose eyes smiled

when he spoke. He had a relaxed, rough exterior and reclined with an arm along the back of the sectional sofa. His petite wife, Talia, sat close to him and was the complete opposite. Chic in an ankle length maxi dress and minimal jewelry, she wore her thick hair piled on top of her head in twists, giving her a refined, almost regal appearance.

Talia headed up the creative services department at Omega Advertising and was Brenda's initial contact on how to incorporate the feature stories about DJ Terror. It was nice to finally put a face to the name.

"You must have some dirt," Tomas continued.

Talia elbowed her husband, and he laughed as if she'd only tapped his stomach with her little finger. "Don't listen to him."

"My lips are sealed." Brenda turned her fingers like a key in front of her mouth, locking her lips. "All the celebrities I work with are great. I love my job. Thank you very much."

A series of disappointed moans went up from the group.

"Brenda knows how to keep a secret," Jay announced from his position in the doorway. "You're wasting your time."

Was that a jab at her?

The black man who had acknowledged her when she arrived, sauntered into the room from the kitchen. He was the media director at Jay's firm. He had pleasant features and a crooked grin. More often than not, she caught his eyes on her.

"Well if you won't give us any dirt on the celebrities," he said, diving into the conversation as if he'd been in the room all along, "give us some dirt on the boss man, here. He can't be as straight-laced as he appears to be."

"Don't get fired in this economy, Terrence," a woman seated to Brenda's left warned.

Terrence laughed. "You've got it all wrong. I'm indispensable, right Jay?"

Jay sipped his wine before answering and frowned in mock deep thought. "We have a saying in Italian. *Se sono rose, fioriranno.*"

"What does that mean?" Terrence asked.

"Time will tell."

Howling and oh's filled the room, but Terrence laughed it off, unperturbed. He and Jay clearly had a good relationship.

Terrence's eyes met Brenda's. "So does that mean there's no dirt? Nothing at all I can use to blackmail him for a raise?"

"You'll have to earn that raise on your own merits. He and I have been friends for a very long time, and he's a fine, upstanding citizen." She didn't look at Jay but felt his eyes on her, and heat warmed her cheeks.

"Aw shucks. Back to the drawing board."

The group laughed and then broke into subgroups of conversation. The games started up again and Brenda became caught up in a vicious game of Uno that involved much trash talking and slamming of cards.

Throughout the night, she observed the interaction between Jay and Helen. Helen appeared, for all intents and purposes, to be co-hosting the party with Jay. She made sure everyone had plenty to eat and drink, pointed individuals in the direction of the bathroom when asked, and greeted late-arriving newcomers.

Despite her helpful behavior, Brenda had the

impression Jay didn't see her as a co-host. He was perfectly polite to Helen in every interaction, but Brenda knew him well enough to know he didn't return Helen's feelings. Every time she cornered him, he found a way to ease away and go back to mingling with his guests, never ignoring a single person.

Every now and again he checked on Brenda. She would look up and he'd smile or sidle his way over and ask if she was okay since she was the only one at the party who didn't know anyone else. Or, he'd squeeze her arm as he walked by, a particularly troublesome act that sent heat shooting to her gut. She'd see the question *Are you okay?* in his eyes, and she smiled to reassure him. She was having a good time with his friends, and being plied with wine and delicious food helped.

She'd already eaten three sliders from the create-your-own slider bar, which had such delicious options as sautéed mushrooms, caramelized onions, and spicy ketchup, along with other fixings. Then there were the prosciutto wrapped melons and tomato and basil crostini. She hadn't even tried the focaccia bread yet but planned to work her way to it before the night was over.

The time passed quickly, and it was well after midnight when the party started winding down and the sound of thunder threatened that a storm was brewing. Little by little, guests left, and by the time the heavy raindrops hit the roof, the only people remaining were Brenda, Helen, Terrence, Tomas, and Talia.

"Here's a picture of our son," Talia said. She leaned from under her husband's arm to share the photo on her phone. A chubby-faced little boy with light café au lait skin and his father's eyes laughed into the camera.

"He's gorgeous," Brenda gushed.

"She didn't want to leave him," Tomas said. An affectionate smile crossed his lips when he looked at his wife. "But I told her there was nothing wrong with going out for a few hours."

Brenda returned the phone to Talia. "I don't blame you for wanting to spend as much time with your son as possible."

"He's in good hands with my best friend," Talia admitted. She turned to her husband. "We should probably go, though, shouldn't we?"

"Yes," he agreed.

They stood and Jay and Helen walked them to the door. Terrence leaned toward Brenda. "I guess I should be leaving, too. Give me a call some time." He extended a business card, but the flirtatious smile he sent her way made it clear he wasn't interested in business only. "Hopefully I'll see you around more often."

"Maybe," she said carefully. She took the card and stood. "I should probably leave, too."

"Brenda, do you have a minute?" Jay asked. "I need some help in the kitchen."

What could she possibly help him with when he had Helen at his disposal? "Excuse me." Brenda eased by Terrence.

In the kitchen, Jay waved her over to where he stood in front of the huge range.

"What's up?" she asked.

"Don't leave," he said in a conspiratorial voice. "At least not yet. I need you to stay so I can get rid of Helen."

Now this was interesting. "You mean Dr. Stafford?"

"Don't make jokes. She's a brilliant scientist with a Ph.D. in molecular biology."

"Then why are you asking me to cock block?" Brenda whispered.

"Is it still called cock blocking when you're trying to block a woman?" he asked in a low tone.

She thought about it. "You know, I'm not sure."

"Anyway, never mind. Will you help me?"

She pursed her lips. "Hmm…what's in it for me?"

His eyes narrowed. "You'll feel good about yourself because you did a nice thing for a friend."

"Nope, that's not enough of an incentive."

"You're evil."

"Still need my help, Mr. Stallion?" Her position of power was immensely satisfying.

Jay groaned. "Fine. You'll leave here with a bottle of wine and several pieces of my secret stash of a *delicious* dessert that I didn't share tonight."

Her ears perked up, like he knew they would. As a fellow gourmand, he knew she couldn't resist the temptation of anything that was even remotely *delicious.* "Did you say dessert?"

His mouth lifted into a smug half-smile. "I did."

"What is it?"

He looked around the room, pretending to make sure no one overheard, and leaned in. She stopped breathing at that very moment.

Standing close like that, she could clearly see his eyes. There were fine lines at the corners, caused by his teasing smile, and the light grey was filled with amusement. She took in the contours of his face, the sloping angle of his narrow nose and the provocative curve of his lips. He truly was a beautiful man—though the adjective was a tad unsuitable for someone so masculine.

"I have three words for you. Espresso chocolate chip brownies."

With difficulty, she found her voice. "That's four words."

"I have four words for you. Espresso chocolate chip brownies."

"Sold!" When he shook his head in mock disgust, she giggled and playfully shoved his arm. Her hand connected with solid muscle, reminding her of the strength concealed under the shirt he filled out so well.

She followed him out to the main room. "I'll see you on Monday, Jay," Terrence said.

"Hold on a minute. Why don't you walk out with Terrence?" he said to Helen.

"Oh, I thought…"

"Brenda's going to stay and help me clean up."

Helen's gaze swung from him to Brenda and back to him.

"That way we can catch up, too, right Jay?" Brenda said.

"That's right. We have a lot to catch up on. So, thanks a lot for all your help tonight." He gave Helen a quick hug and then gently pushed her toward the door.

"Bye, Brenda, it was nice to meet you." Frowning, Helen craned her neck to get a last look at Brenda, confusion evident on her face.

"Likewise." Brenda waved.

Jay shut the door. Leaning his back against it, he breathed a loud sigh of relief. Then he smiled apologetically at her. "Sorry about that."

"Are you really?"

"Not really."

With everyone gone, the house was ominously quiet. She and Jay, alone. That hadn't happened in a very, very long time.

She placed both hands on her hips. "Do I really have to help you clean up?"

"I could use a hand," he said.

"Lucky for you, I have two." She held them up.

Brenda and Jay worked together mostly in quiet, with Jay giving directions every now and again. They cleaned the living room, tossing disposable cups and plates in the trash. He folded the card table and chairs and stored them in a closet down the hall. When he went into the kitchen to put away leftovers, she vacuumed. He came back into the room and they rearranged the furniture, and then she joined him in the kitchen and helped there. She washed dishes while he dried and put them away. Pretty soon, the kitchen was clean and clear of debris, as if he hadn't had about twenty people in his house tonight.

Hands on hips, Brenda surveyed their work. "We did good."

Jay nodded. "Not bad."

Rain continued to fall in a steady torrent, and Brenda eyed the water running down the windows. "I hate driving in the rain this time of night."

"Then don't." Jay shrugged. "Hang out here until it dies down."

Silence fell between them as she twisted his suggestion around in her head. Sticking around a little longer couldn't hurt.

"Are you sure? You don't have to go to sleep or

anything?"

"Not at all. I'm wide awake." He faced her from across the kitchen, gripping the countertop behind him. He spoke in a laid back tone, but his eyes rested on her with an unusual watchfulness that made her feel like a fly caught in a spider web.

She twisted her hands together. "If you're sure…"

"I'm sure, Brenda." Slight irritation colored his voice. "It's late, and I'd rather you wait out the rain at this time of night."

She felt silly. There was absolutely no reason why she and Jay couldn't be alone, and she'd really rather wait until the rain at least subsided. "Okay." She lifted one shoulder in a nonchalant shrug and took a deep, silent breath. "I'll…I'll stay, then."

CHAPTER FIVE

The scent of freshly brewed coffee wafted out from the kitchen. Normally the aroma enticed her, but Brenda fidgeted in the living room, unable to find a comfortable position on the perfectly comfortable sofa. She should have left with Terrence and Helen and would have, if she hadn't been so greedy. A plastic sack with the bottle of wine and two brownies mocked her from the table.

But not only greed had kept her there. Something else had, too—something she didn't want to acknowledge. She and Jay hadn't been alone together, with not another soul around them, in a long, long time. Not since...

Brenda sprang from the sofa, gnawing her bottom lip.

Staying was a bad idea. Even if Jay didn't think it was a bad idea, she certainly did. She would make an excuse for why she should leave right this minute. She could always pull over on the side of the road and wait out the storm if necessary.

Jay came out of the kitchen carrying a tray with two mugs of coffee and two small white plates, each with a square of rich-looking brownie on it.

"There you go." He placed the tray on the table. "A brownie and coffee, black the way you like it." They both drank their coffee the same way—no sugar, no cream.

Her resolve wavered. He was being so gracious, and what would it hurt to stay a few more minutes? And it was still raining pretty hard. Better safe than sorry.

"I'm not going to take your wine," she informed him, lowering onto the sofa.

"Take it. I promised you wine, and you more than held up your end of the bargain."

He sprawled in the seat across from her, a cushy armchair with narrow blue and white stripes. His long legs stretched out in front of him. He seemed relaxed and very much at ease. His defined muscles under the shirt caught her gaze, but she steered her eyes away and to the food on the table.

"Okay, I'll take the wine. Since you're twisting my arm," she said.

"That didn't take much," Jay said in an amused voice.

Brenda sipped the coffee, listening to the rain pelt the windows and the roof, a steady attack that didn't sound as if it would let up anytime soon.

"We should get together more often," Jay said. He picked up his mug of coffee and took a sip.

"We should. All of us."

He set his mug on the table beside him where a lamp illuminated one side of his face. He didn't respond or react to her suggestion.

"So you really like your job?" he asked.

"I love it, and I'm glad I'm back in Atlanta."

"Being an entertainment editor suits you."

"Oh really? What does that mean?"

He cocked his head, eyes narrowing. "You're a people person. You ever thought about acting?"

"No way!"

"Why not? You have the personality for that, too, I think." He studied her with a thoughtful gaze.

"And what kind of personality is that?" She pinched a corner from the brownie and ate it. Delicious. She moaned quietly to herself, tasting the espresso and the chocolate, a potent combination that had her in dessert heaven.

A slow, knowing smile formed on his lips. "Good?"

"Mhmm." So good, she picked up the plate and sliced into the dessert with the fork.

"Okay, what kind of personality is that…" Jay steepled his fingers. He seemed in deep thought, which amused her. "Actually, I have no idea what kind of personality that takes. I assume it takes someone who's outgoing and friendly." He shrugged.

"First of all, thank you for that compliment."

"You're welcome." He inclined his head in a pretend salute to her.

Brenda slipped another piece of brownie into her mouth. After she'd swallowed, she said, "I wasn't entirely truthful when you asked me about my interest in acting. You want to know a secret?"

"Sure." His eyes filled with curiosity.

She'd never told anyone this before. "I used to want to be an actress. Even took classes. I imagined myself on stage or on screen like my favorite stars."

"What happened?" He was frowning now.

She'd seen acting as a way to escape a tacky life with a single mother who embarrassed her with tawdry behavior, and a sister who became her responsibility simply because Brenda was eleven years older. The classes had been ridiculously cheap and offered by a former stage director at the community center near her home. For an entire year she'd saved the meager allowance her father sent, and when the classes started, she'd taken her sister with her twice a week for the one-hour sessions.

"I took the classes and..." Brenda took a deep breath and stared down at the almost empty plate. She'd eaten more of the brownie than she realized.

It was so long ago but it still hurt a little. When you're fifteen years old and want something so bad, when you see it as your escape from the distastefulness of your immediate environment, the words of someone you admire can cut deep.

"I took the classes, and at the end of the course, the director told me I didn't have what it takes to be an actress."

"Why the hell not?" Jay sat up with a start, offended on her behalf. She appreciated his passionate response.

"He said I was too much." Her cheeks and neck burned from embarrassment.

"Too much? What does that mean?"

"He said I overdid every scene, overdramatized the dialogue and my actions. That I was an...over-actor."

"Oh." Jay settled back into the chair. His response was very comical, as if he agreed with the director. She broke into a fit of laughter.

The fact that she'd held onto this secret for so long, as if it somehow defined her, was ridiculous. Holding onto the secret had given the incident much more power than it deserved.

"He was right, too," she said in between laughs. "I sucked at acting."

Jay laughed and covered his mouth with a fist. "I can see that. You can be very dramatic."

"*Shut up.*" She tossed one of the pillows at him.

He easily caught it and set it on the floor beside him. "See what I mean?"

When they stopped laughing, she looked across the room at him and smiled. "I'm doing what I should be doing and right where I should be," she said.

Instead of becoming an actor, she became someone who chronicled the highs and lows of their lives. But she admired their skill and the sacrifice—though others may not see it that way—they made to pursue a career in the public eye.

"I think you're right. You're right where you should be," Jay said.

His steady gaze hinted at a deeper meaning behind the words. At the mild uptick in her pulse, Brenda's eyes skittered away from his to look out the window. The rain had eased up enough that she couldn't hear it anymore. Still, she stayed put.

"I think Terrence is interested in you," Jay said.

"I think so, too." She wanted to start dating again but didn't think dating someone who worked for Jay was a good idea. She picked up the coffee. "What's the story with you and Helen?" she asked carefully. Her pulse beat a little faster, apprehensive about his response.

"I thought it was obvious. There is no story."

"You're being mean." She looked up at him. "You know she's interested in you. It's so obvious."

Jay shook his head and tapped the arm of the chair. "She's a friend who wants more, but a relationship wouldn't work between us."

"Why not?"

"She's not Italian."

"What does that have to do with anything?"

"My father insists that's why my marriage didn't last. Because my wife wasn't Italian. I've been advised that the next time I marry, I should marry a nice Italian woman." He grimaced.

"Parents are something else, aren't they?" Jay had as much parental drama as she did. Her mother constantly embarrassed her, and his father never approved of anything he did. "Your father sounds almost like my mother."

"How so?"

"When she found out I was moving back to Atlanta, she was happy because there are a lot of quote, successful black men, unquote, here. She hopes I'll find a good black man and finally get married."

Jay stopped tapping the furniture and his body grew very still. His gaze fixed on her. "Is that what you want?"

"To get married? Sure." She'd actually thought she would be married by now. Finding the right man was taking longer than she'd expected.

"Does your husband have to be black?"

She'd never really thought about it much, but the question was easy to answer. Nowadays, people had options and fewer concerns about societal approval, unlike the days when her neighbor, Mrs. Chen, had met and married her husband. "No, he doesn't have to be black."

Jay resumed tapping the arm of the chair.

"What about you?" Brenda asked. "Do you have a preference?"

"No. I'd like to be married again, though." His answer surprised her. She assumed Jay had so much fun dating, marriage was not a priority. "I don't care what she looks like."

"So five hundred pounds, a unibrow, and a beard would work?"

His shoulders shook with laughter. "That's not really my type, but…"

"But you'd give her a shot?"

"I'd give anyone a shot." She didn't even want to examine why his response was a relief and why she breathed easier because of it. His choice of future wife had no bearing on her personal situation.

He lifted his coffee and held it out toward her. "Here's to finding happiness with someone. No matter what they look like or where they're from."

She lifted her cup, too. "Agreed."

The toast signaled the end of their conversation. She finished her coffee and Jay removed the empty dishes to the kitchen before walking her out to the car. Standing beside the Jetta on the dark street, there were no lights on in most of the houses, and the neighborhood was quiet except for a dog barking several doors down.

Brenda shifted the plastic bag with the goodies he'd given her from her left to right hand. "Guess I'll be sleeping late tomorrow." She faked a yawn, ready to break away before awkwardness descended between them.

"Thank you for staying and all your help." Jay pulled her into an unexpected, one-armed hug. "I had a good time," he murmured. He held his mouth close to her ear, his beard brushing her skin.

She froze, turning into a stiff column, even as heat and arousal merged between her thighs. She kept one hand between them so they didn't get too close. "I had a good time, too," she mumbled.

She tried to withdraw, but his hold tightened by a fraction, enough to keep her in the embrace. His splayed out fingers ran up and down her spine, and her body became even more rigid. The way he brushed his hands over her back sent a wave of heat to wash down her body. This was a man touching a woman, not a friend touching a friend.

Flattening her hand against his chest and gently pushing, she made an effort to break free again. This time he lifted his other hand to her arm. He had to know she was trying to get away from him, but she was at a mild disadvantage with one hand still holding the bag of brownies and wine.

"Good night, Brenda." He placed a soft kiss on her cheek. A chaste, innocent kiss that didn't feel chaste, didn't feel innocent coming from him. Not when his mouth was moist and the rough hairs of his beard scuffed her cheek and made her throb with want.

She shoved hard against his chest and bounced half a car length away from him. Oddly enough, she missed the closeness and his touch, even while she acknowledged guilt for craving those things.

"Why did you do that?" she demanded. Her pulse had elevated, beating fast at her temple and the base of her neck.

"It was just a—"

"Don't act as if you don't know what you did. As if it was nothing."

He shoved his fingers through his hair, chest visibly lifting with labored breathing.

His face tightened. "Why did *I* do that? Why do *you* do that?" He shook his head and laughed, a humorless and angry sound. "Why do you always act as if my touch is the worst, most disgusting, most horrible thing you could imagine?"

"You shouldn't have kissed me!"

"Maybe I couldn't help myself!" he shot back. He let out a heavy breath and fell back against the car, scraping his fingers through his hair again. "Maybe I'm an asshole and not a fine, upstanding citizen," he said in a tired voice.

Closing her eyes briefly, Brenda gathered the resolve necessary to leave. When she lifted her lids, he was staring at her. She didn't know what he thought. Nor did she care. He'd crossed a line.

"Goodnight, Jay." Her voice should have been firm, but it came out soft and throaty.

A defeated slump to his shoulders, he stepped away from the car, giving her plenty of room. She edged to the driver door. Fumbling, she attempted to put the key in the hole, failing to accomplish the task three times while he watched. She finally opened the door and hopped in, eyes averted from his silent figure.

She started the car and made a U-turn, driving away without acknowledging him but lifting her eyes to the rearview mirror just the same. Jay stood in the wet road, feet spread apart, arms hanging loosely at his sides. Dressed in all black with black hair and black shoes, he looked more like a shadow than a person standing there. He remained in the same spot even after she turned onto the next street.

Brenda breathed easier once he was out of sight. Her muscles relaxed and the heat in her abdomen subsided. Being alone with Jay was never, ever a good idea, and she wouldn't make the same mistake again.

She tightened her hands on the steering wheel and focused on the road ahead. She couldn't wait to get home and as far away from Jacopo Santorini as possible.

CHAPTER SIX

His staff hated Friday meetings, and hated them even more on sunny afternoons in June, but Jay couldn't wait to give them the good news.

"We're having another great quarter." The seven-member executive team seated around the glass conference table clapped and cheered. "The creative services department continues to do an incredible job with the ad campaigns and image rebranding. Feedback from our clients through the surveys continues to be overwhelmingly positive. Special thanks to Talia and her team for an outstanding job." He inclined his head toward the only female in the room, and everyone clapped.

Talia smiled her appreciation at the public acknowledgement.

Jay then went down the list, complimenting the media buying department for negotiating impressive discounts, account services for excellent customer service, and finance for keeping everyone within budget. "Good job everybody," he said when the clapping had died down. "Now get your asses back to work."

Chuckles filled the room, and the group filed out, talking amongst themselves. Jay was the last to leave. He stopped in the break room and filled a cup with herbal tea before heading back to his office. He passed his executive assistant's empty desk, went into his office and closed the door. The first thing he did was call his father, Gino Santorini, in Italy and give him the same update as the staff.

Gino had retired from the company years ago and, concerned about Jay's playboy ways, hadn't expected it to run so smoothly under Jay's leadership. Ironic, considering his father hadn't been faithful to Jay's mother during their marriage and regularly traveled the world with his latest girlfriend. Yet he'd handed over the reins of his successful advertising firm, and to put his father's mind at ease, he kept him abreast of goings on at the firm.

Thirty minutes later, he was signing contracts when his secretary called.

"Yes?"

"Your ex-wife is on the phone."

Jay slammed the pen on the pile of papers. She still had the power to spoil his day with a single phone call. "Put her through."

The line went silent, and when the call was passed through, he greeted his ex-wife. "Hello, Jenna."

"I hope you don't mind my calling," she said.

"How can I help you?" His tone was scrap-the-bullshit sharp. She knew how much he disliked taking personal calls at work, yet she frequently called during business hours. That was typical of her, though. She didn't care if her desire to have or do something inconvenienced other people. He supposed such behavior was the result of being doted on by an indulgent father.

"Marco's been acting up in summer camp," she said, sounding tired and frustrated. "Could you call him later and talk to him about his behavior?"

Jay's eyes found the framed picture of Arturo and Marco on his desk, a year-old shot taken at a studio and sent to him for Father's Day last year. They both wore suits and playful expressions. Arturo had dark hair and swarthy skin like Jay and most members of their southern Italian family. Marco, on the other hand, was a paler-skinned, towheaded youngster who took after his mother.

"What did he do?"

"He mouthed off to one of the counselors a few days ago and was excluded from activities for the rest of the day. Then today the director called to say he was in a fight with another boy."

Jay frowned. That didn't sound like his son. For the most part, Marco was a gentle kid. "Why was he fighting?"

"The boy called him fat, and *your* son punched him. The director said the next thing she knew, they were rolling around on the ground. Marco claims the boy threw the first punch, but the boy said Marco hit him first. None of the other kids actually saw the fight start. If Marco acts up again, they're kicking him out of the program."

Jay rubbed his bristled jaw. "It's tough with him going though that chubby phase. I told him he'll outgrow it, but he wants to look more like Arturo." On top of the insecurities about his body, Marco struggled with colorblindness. The inability to see shades of red and green was a disability that added to his son's misery.

"I understand, but we can't tolerate this type of behavior. I don't know what to do with him anymore," Jenna said.

If he was standing up for himself when bullied, Jay found it hard to be angry.

"Are you there?" Jenna asked, sounding even more frustrated.

"Yes, I'm here. I'll talk to him."

"Tonight? They're allowed to get phone calls at the end of the day."

"I'll call him before I leave work," he promised.

"Don't forget."

Jay gritted his teeth. She took such pleasure in schooling him about being a parent, yet whenever she felt out of her depth with the boys, she didn't hesitate to call.

"I won't. Anything else?"

Silence.

Impatiently, Jay tapped the pen on a stack of papers. He didn't have time to dawdle on the phone with Jenna. He had to finish reading and signing these contracts. Then he had to write a memo to the account executives on revisions to the company's best practices for handling problem clients. All this plus drive thirty miles to a client's pre-opening restaurant party they'd begged him to attend.

"Are you doing okay?" Jenna asked.

Jay stopped tapping. She seldom expressed concern about his well-being. There were times he wondered if she'd ever loved him at all. "I'm fine."

"Good."

She fell quiet again, and while the silence was

nerve-wracking enough to want to get off the phone, he didn't speak until she did.

"I'm seeing someone. It's kind of serious and…I thought I'd mention it."

He hadn't expected her to divulge that type of information and wasn't sure how he felt. "Oh?"

"I told the boys about him and I'm introducing them to each other this weekend. We're all going out to dinner."

Jay didn't begrudge his ex-wife the opportunity to date. He certainly did—all manner of women from all walks of life. The women were interchangeable and most didn't last long enough to make an impression. He could barely remember their personalities, and even their physical traits blurred together at times.

In all the years since the divorce, he'd never known Jenna to date anyone seriously. At least not seriously enough to introduce to the boys. He didn't love her anymore, but she was the mother of his children, a link that made him curious about her new beau.

"Who is he? Do I know him?"

"Do you remember Dale Armstrong? He attended our wedding. We've always been friends, but he and I started dating recently, after he and his wife divorced."

He vaguely remembered meeting Dale, but the memory was a fuzzy one.

"You don't even care, do you?" Jenna asked. His lack of response had made her angry.

Jay rubbed his forehead. He'd better diffuse the situation right away or she'd have a meltdown. "I want you to be happy. You moving on doesn't affect me, except I want Dale to treat my sons with care and respect. As long as he doesn't mistreat them, I'll be fine."

"He won't."

"Then we should be fine."

"Thank you," she said quietly.

He flipped through the pages of the next contract he had to sign. "Well, I have to—"

"Do you ever wonder if things could have been different between us?" Jenna asked.

Jay pinched his nose. He didn't want to go there. Rather than answer truthfully, he asked, "Different how?"

"I don't know. Just...different. You know, if you could have loved me the way that I loved you." She laughed hollowly. "Maybe we could have been happy and still married. Our lives would have certainly been different. A lot of things would have been different. But of course, you can't make someone love you. Not any more than you can stop loving someone, can you?" That was a loaded question for sure.

"You enjoy blaming the collapse of our marriage on me, but you're the one who gave up," he reminded her. "You're the one who wouldn't let me touch you. You're the one who left."

"Why would I let you touch me?" Jenna asked, in a quietly bitter voice. "When you were thinking of someone else?"

"There was no one else," he grated. "Saying it doesn't make it true. I was faithful to you during our marriage. You gave up."

"I gave up because I accepted that even though I was your wife and I had given you sons, and you were physically faithful, emotionally you were cheating on me. You didn't love me. You didn't have any passion for me. I was a—a substitute for the person you really wanted."

His neck muscles tightened under the effort to remain calm. "This is a ridiculous conversation. Did you call to rehash the same old arguments again?"

"You've never denied it!" Jenna screeched. "Not once have you ever denied your heart was elsewhere. Not once have you ever said that you loved me."

"I loved you. You know I loved you."

"But you weren't *in* love with me. Who was she, Jay?"

He lowered his voice and spoke between clenched teeth. "If you're so certain there was someone else, why am I still alone?"

"I can't answer that question. By choice, maybe. Although you sleep around plenty, so your bed is never empty."

He'd much rather wake up next to the same woman every day, but he'd grown accustomed to seeking comfort in the arms of different women. Thanks to her, his ego had taken a bruising during their short marriage, and she damn well knew it.

"I have to get back to work." Cutting the conversation short was the best tactic and one he often employed to handle her. Otherwise, they'd end up in a shouting match.

"Yes, get back to work, Jacopo. Don't let me keep you from your precious job, which is so much more important than our boring conversation." She slammed down the phone and he winced from the explosive sound.

Jay placed the receiver in the cradle and stifled the urge to yell out loud in frustration. Instead, he slammed his fist on top of the desk.

She'd had an agenda today for sure. She'd wanted to rub his nose in her relationship, but there was something else she wanted to tell him, too. There had been enough hesitation in her voice, an underlying *something* that made him wonder if she'd said all she intended to.

A knock came at the door. Another interruption he didn't need.

"Come in," he called.

Terrence appeared. "Hey Jay, can I talk to you for a minute?"

Jay waved him in. "Sure, come on in."

Terrence took a seat in the guest chair and placed an ankle over his knee. "So, your lady friend from game night—Brenda. Is she seeing anyone?"

Jay stiffened. "Why do you ask?"

"Because I'm interested." He sat forward on the edge of the chair. "She's funny, sexy, cute, and we had a good conversation at your house. At least I think so. Thought we had chemistry, but I gave her my number and she never called. Then I thought, what if she lost my card? So I figured maybe you could find out—"

"She's seeing someone."

Terrence straightened. "She is? I could have sworn she was single."

Terrence exemplified the type of man Brenda's mother hoped she'd meet in Atlanta. *A good black man.*

"That's incorrect," Jay said shortly. He didn't experience a lick of remorse for lying. "It's been a while since you've seen her, remember? Four, five weeks. Something like that."

Terrence looked deflated. "You think it's serious already?"

"I don't know, but it wouldn't be a very good idea

to set up an employee with one of my friends." His voice dripped ice.

Terrence's eyebrows elevated. "Oh, okay. I understand. Huh. Thanks for your time." He rose from the chair and headed out of the office but paused at the door. "She is just a friend, right?" He walked out without waiting for an answer.

Jay sat back in the chair and rubbed his jaw. He didn't give a shit what Terrence thought. He wasn't the least bit sorry he'd shot him down because he ran an advertising firm. Not a goddamn dating service.

CHAPTER SEVEN

Cameras flashed and the sound of applause filled the air as Claudine James, actress on the big and small screen, hoisted a glass of champagne in the air and toasted the audience in celebration. Next to Claudine, Chef Bijoux raised her own glass. Both women grinned at each other, brimming with pride at the evening's outcome.

Jay secured an invite to the pre-opening event because Omega Advertising helped launch the restaurant, the third in the past two years from a group of investors that placed their celebrity partners out front to garner as much publicity as possible.

Nestled along a tree-lined street in Midtown, the upscale dining establishment was filled with well-wishers, taking a peek at the business marriage between the famous actress and Chef Bijoux, from the Food Network. Stark white linens covered the tables, and the dark wood-paneled walls in the main dining room lent an intimacy that caused the gathered crowd to speak in hushed tones. The assortment of dishes circulated by the servers was a variation of the Southern comfort food the actress had grown up eating, able to satisfy even the most discerning palate.

Jay set his empty plate on one of the tables strategically placed around the dining room floor. He'd practically licked it clean. Minutes before the small dish had been filled with fried green tomatoes garnished with goat cheese and a drizzle of basil aioli.

Now that the festivities were almost over he could leave, confident in the success of another one of their projects. He ambled toward the exit, winding his way between the media people and other invitees, when he caught sight of Brenda over near the wall. He should have known she'd be here.

His footsteps slowed to a halt and he just stood there, taking her in. Dressed in a pair of charcoal slacks, white ruffled shirt with pearl buttons, and a charcoal blazer, she talked animatedly to one of the food critics for the local newspaper. She made sweeping gestures with her hands and used energetic nods to agree with the man's comments.

At one point she laughed, and even though he couldn't hear her, his stomach clenched just the same because he knew the sound. Relished it. Missed it.

When her eyes landed on Jay, her expansive movements stopped. After a brief hesitation she acknowledged him with a faint smile. He smiled back and leaned against the wall to wait for her.

He didn't have long to wait. A couple of minutes later, she excused herself and walked across the carpeted floor to his side. Her soft, sweet fragrance enveloped him, and he stuffed his hands into his pockets to suppress the sudden urge to pull her into his arms. Last time that didn't go so well.

"Don't tell me, this is you?" She waved in the general direction of the restaurant and guests.

"We had a hand in the launch, yes. The investors are our clients."

"I should have known."

"I thought the same thing when I saw you." Damn, she looked good up close. Nude-colored lipstick made her already full lips appear plumper and moist. Tonight she'd done something to make her hair wavy and combed it back from her face. He liked the new style.

"I've been getting out more now that I'm settled at the magazine. I guess we'll be seeing each other more often at events around town."

"Probably." *Maledizione*, they couldn't even talk to each other. Their conversation sounded fake and unnatural—nothing like two people who'd known each other for years.

She clasped her hands in front of her. "Well, it was good to see you. I'd better go."

"Brenda," he said, as she was walking away. She turned back to face him. "Listen, the last time we saw each other…" He sighed. "Do you think we could go somewhere to talk? We've known each other a long time, and I—I don't want to lose your friendship."

She eyed him warily, probably suspicious of his intentions. "I don't want to lose your friendship, either," she said cautiously. "Where did you have in mind?"

"There's a place on Peachtree, not too far from where I work. It's a little wine bar I visit often to unwind after work. We could go there, have a drink, and talk."

"Okay." She nodded. "That sounds like a good

idea."

He breathed a little easier. "We could park in the lot near the office." He took a look at her shoes, black peep-toe pumps. "You'll be okay walking the three or so blocks to the bar in those?"

"I'll be fine," she said, brushing off his concern with a wave of her hand. "What's the name of the wine bar?"

"Vino Luogo," he answered.

A hint of a smile appeared at the corners of her luscious mouth. "Surprise, surprise. Of course it's Italian."

"Of course. They have a variety of wines, but you'll never taste a better selection than what's available on their Italian list."

Brenda groaned, already loosening up. "You Italians and your food and wine bragging. You actually believe you have the best wine in the world, don't you?"

He shot her his best appalled look. "That's because we do."

"Sorry to disappoint you," she teased, "but the best wine I've ever had wasn't Italian. It was a California red—fruity and textured with hints of cedar and cardamom. *Delicious.*"

"You must be joking," he muttered. "Your unsophisticated American palate doesn't know any better, so I forgive your blasphemy."

Brenda laughed, cute and sexy at the same time. A sound he would never get tired of, even when she was giving him hell. "Oh please. Italian wines are good, don't get me wrong—but there are so many good ones out there, I have to say that Italian wine is one among many."

"You'll eat those words," he promised.

"You're serious, aren't you?"

"Yes." Their playful banter had recharged him, and the thought of spending time with her tipped his pulse rate forward a little faster.

"Okay, Mr. Santorini, let's go." She walked ahead of him.

His gaze dropped, admiring the left-right swing of her hips.

At the door Brenda cast a glance over her shoulder and almost caught him staring at her behind. "This better be some damn good wine."

"It is," he assured her. He opened the door and let her precede him. "Trust me."

****

If she hadn't been with Jay, Brenda would have walked right past Vino Luogo, almost hidden in plain sight with a nondescript glass door and nestled between two businesses on either side.

"Mr. Santorini." The host, a middle-aged man with a portly build and bushy dark beard greeted Jay.

"Hello, Joel."

"I see you have a guest tonight. Give me a few minutes to find you a table." He lumbered away.

"You weren't kidding," Brenda murmured to Jay. "You really do come here often."

"I'm afraid so," he said with a small smile.

Vino Luogo was indeed 'a little wine bar,' like Jay said. Dark furniture and dimmed lights created a cozy atmosphere. Shaped like a long rectangle, the dining room contained small tables lining the walls, none able to seat more than four people, the majority accommodating two. A low hum of conversation filled the packed room. If Joel found a free table, it

71

would be a miracle.

Apparently, miracles do happen. He found a two-top near the back in a semi-quiet corner against the exposed brick wall. Brenda hadn't planned to eat again, but the small plate menu featured intriguing choices such as edamame hummus and bacon popcorn. She broke down and let Jay suggest a few items for them to nosh on.

They opted for the bacon popcorn, set in the center for sharing, and a plate of mushroom flatbread for Brenda. Jay chose tomato flatbread with fontina cheese and a drizzle of balsamic reduction. Not long after the food arrived, the waiter poured them each a glass of Nebbiolo wine and set the half-empty carafe on the table.

Brenda picked up the bowl-shaped stemware.

"*Salute,*" Jay said.

He watched her as she swirled the liquid and lowered her nose to inhale its fragrance. "Mmmm." She took a sip and allowed the wine to roll over her tongue. Full-bodied with complex flavors and notes of licorice, it was arguably the best red she'd ever tasted.

Across the table from her, Jay wore a self-satisfied smirk. "I won't ask what you think because I already have a pretty good idea."

He did know wines. "When you're right, you're right." She set the glass on the table.

He leaned toward her, a glint of amusement in his eye. "You can thank me now."

She rolled her eyes and said one of only a handful of Italian words that she knew. "*Grazie.*"

Jay watched her with a pleased expression on his face, before lifting his glass and taking a sip.

She slipped a morsel of cubed flatbread into her mouth, concentrating on the task and the flavor of the caramelized mushrooms. Anything but look across the table at him and the way his mouth closed over the glass.

"How is your sister?" he asked.

Her sister Tracey would start her last year of college in the fall. "She's fine. We spoke last week. Her studies are coming along well."

"What's her major again?"

"Computer information systems."

"Ah yes. Good for her." He twirled the glass on the table.

For a long time, neither said a word. Her gaze flitted over the rest of the diners seated at the small tables and the curved, wooden tasting bar. Mostly couples, but there were also small groups of friends, and from the private room a bachelorette party's cheering and clapping could be heard.

"I'm sorry," Jay said.

Her attention came back to him. She almost missed the quiet apology. Her heart constricted a little, saddened they'd come to this point. "I'm sorry, too. I overreacted."

"You didn't overreact." He made the statement in a matter-of-fact way and then drank some wine. He set the glass carefully on the table but his eyes remained trained on it. He frowned, as if searching the depths for the answer to a question. "You seeing anyone?" Now, he studied her with the same intensity he had the wine.

"Uh...n-no, I'm not," she stuttered. The change in topic threw her. "Not right now."

"No broken hearts left behind in Chicago?"

"Plural? No way?" She laughed, albeit uneasily. Conversations like this, particularly with Jay of all people, always made her uneasy. "There was someone, but he doesn't have a broken heart, I assure you. We cut ties when I left. It wasn't very serious." She picked up a kernel of corn from the bowl in the center of the table and slipped it into her mouth. Jay hadn't eaten anything since they sat down.

"Not serious for you." Not even the hint of a smile was on his face, attentive eyes capturing every word and every movement.

"Not for either of us." She wanted to change the subject and avoided his eyes, focusing on a still life painting of wine bottles and grapes on the wall. When she swung her gaze back to Jay, he was staring at her. "What?" she asked sharply.

"Nothing. Just thinking."

"About what?"

"The past."

He looked at her in a way he never had before, or rather in a way she hadn't seen in a very long time. Her chest felt heavy and she swallowed hard.

"What are you thinking about the past?" A dangerous question, and yet she still asked.

He traced a finger around the rim of his glass. The movement reminded her of an intimate caress, the warm stroke of a lover's fingertip over heated skin.

"Thinking about when Nick introduced you to us he was probably halfway in love with you by then. *Ti ricordi?*"

She looked down at the table, embarrassed.

"Yes, I remember," she answered. "Except for the part about Nick being halfway in love with me."

"You like to pretend it's not true, but he did have

feelings for you. Still does." His voice had dropped lower, almost hypnotizing in its monotony.

Shrugging, she broke eye contact. The line of conversation about Nick made her uncomfortable.

"Did you know he talked about you a lot before he introduced you to us? He mentioned this beautiful woman he wanted us to meet."

She didn't know this little bit of information. Nick had approached her in a cafe. She'd been eating lunch alone while reviewing notes for a class, and he'd walked up and introduced himself. She'd shot him down right away, but eventually they exchanged numbers when he convinced her all he wanted was friendship.

"I don't understand why we're talking about this." Brenda rubbed the back of her neck, wishing she hadn't inquired about his thoughts after all.

Jay stopped tracing the rim of the glass. "Then *I* met you. The night we met, Jenna was with me. *Ti ricordi?*"

"Of course I remember. It was really cold that night. I almost canceled but changed my mind because I'd promised Nick I'd go." They'd met at a popular jazz and blues lounge in Marietta.

"You wore a black sweater dress, knee-high, black leather boots, and a red scarf. Three inch heels. Big dangly gold earrings with diamond accents. A gold ring on the middle finger of your right hand with the design of a rose on it. Pink nail polish. Red lipstick. Your hair was a little longer then, and you had pulled it back from your face."

Brenda swallowed at the amount of detail he recounted.

A bittersweet smile lined his mouth. "I can't

remember what I wore that night. I can't remember what Jenna wore. But I remember every detail of your outfit. I remember what your mouth looked like, your eyes, and especially your smile. I even remember the way you smelled. And I remember thinking..." His voice became quieter, husky. She waited, breathing suspended. "Thinking...that I wish I'd met you first."

A shaky breath expelled from her lungs. The glass in front of her became the center of her attention for a long time. Silence hovered over the table like a gloomy specter.

"Jay..." She risked a look at him, and the intensity in his eyes burned into her soul. This was why they couldn't be alone together, not even in a public place, apparently. "That's the wine talking," she croaked.

His lips firmed, rebellious in the dismissal of her words. "It's the truth."

"You can't say something like that and just..."

"Just what?"

"Not expect me to react." Anger swelled inside of her. Anger that he'd dared say something so intimate, so *wrong*. "You and I can't happen. You know we can't. It wouldn't feel right."

"It would feel right," he said in a measured tone. His gaze raked over her, mentally stripping her naked, violating her with the blatant hunger in his eyes. "It would feel fucking incredible."

She squeezed her thighs together. "Stop it, Jay."

"Why?" he asked harshly. He leaned forward, staring her right in the eyes. "So we can continue to act like there's nothing between us?"

"There *is* nothing between us. It's not an act."

Angry color tinged his cheeks. "Dammit, Brenda, it's been twelve years. Whatever sense of honor or guilt you feel is misplaced."

"Why?" she whispered fiercely. Her eyes shot to the table beside them. Certain the couple wasn't paying them any attention, she continued. "Why did you ask me to come here? So you could harass me? So you could bombard me with your despicable thoughts? Jenna is my friend. I'm not going to betray her because it's convenient for you."

"Jenna and I have been divorced for ten years."

"That doesn't make it right. I don't want to have this conversation with you."

"Tell me you feel nothing."

"Stop it." What they'd done was wrong. He'd had a girlfriend. His girlfriend was her friend.

"Tell me you feel nothing. You can't, because you do. That night—"

"*No.*" She stiffened. The fist in her lap tightened. "We agreed nothing happened. And please, please stop looking at me like that." His eyes said it all. What he wanted to do to her. How he'd do it.

"How long are you going to keep this up?" he asked.

"I'm ready to go," she said, holding his gaze. "You can leave with me or I can leave without you. Whichever you prefer." She picked up the goblet from the table and downed the last of the wine. Her hands shook. Erratic breaths sputtered from her chest.

A stretch of silence hung between them like angry live wire. After a moment's hesitation, Jay also finished off his wine. He called over the waiter and very rudely demanded the check. The poor waiter hadn't done anything wrong but had become a casualty of their tense conversation.

When the bill was paid, Brenda quickly stood and stalked ahead of Jay, not even pausing when he stopped to chat with Joel. She hurried down the street, brushing past the many pedestrians congregated on the city's sidewalks this time of night.

The pleasant evening she'd hoped to enjoy was over. Done. This was her punishment for wanting to spend time with him. Her punishment for enjoying his company too much.

Brenda banked the corner toward the lot where she'd parked her car. She didn't know how close he was until his voice came from behind her.

"Do you plan to keep on running forever?"

She pivoted and faced his angry glare. He loomed over her, appearing even larger than usual because of the street's downward slope.

"It was a kiss. Only a kiss, and a very long time ago. What do you want from me?"

"Honesty. It was more than a kiss," he said, halfway yelling. "Did you forget you were straddling me?"

"Lower your voice." Her eyes darted around the almost empty side street. A man rode by on a bike and a car horn blared, prompting a woman to hustle across the street. "You pulled me on top of your lap. You forced me to straddle you."

Considering all the sidewalk available to him, Jay stepped way too close. "Did I force you to open the buttons on my shirt?"

No, he hadn't done that. Her hands, with minds of their own, had accomplished the task swiftly and with noteworthy gusto.

"Did I force you to lick my chest and neck?"

No, he hadn't done that, either. Her tongue had

taken charge, savoring the distinctive tang of his skin and playing with his hard nipples.

"That was—" Her lips trembled. "I didn't mean to." She blinked rapidly, overcome by the stinging sensation in her chest as he edged even closer.

"*Maledizione*, do you know how long it took for me to forget the scent of you on my fingers?" he asked in a coarse voice. "Do you have any idea how long it took for me to forget how the inside of your mouth tasted?"

She had a good idea, because she'd fought to forget the salty flavor of his skin, the scent of his masculine musk, and the way the inside of *his* mouth tasted.

"Why are you doing this? Why now?" she asked huskily.

"Because it's been twelve years." His voice sounded as if he had an obstruction in his larynx. "Because Charlie is dead and he thought he had time, and the truth is, we don't have time, and we don't know what could happen tomorrow. You said don't put off until tomorrow what can be done today. So I'm not. Having you here in Atlanta, so close but still so far away, has been hard for me. *Giorno e notte penso solo a te.*" He scraped his fingers through the hair on his head. "Every day and every night, you're all I think about."

"Jenna's still in love with you, Jay."

"She's not in love with me! That's the excuse you use to keep away from me. You want me. I want you."

"You can't have me."

"Then I will eventually go crazy. Because ever since you and I—"

"Don't bring it up!" She lifted her hands in protest. "For you to even say something like that—to tell me that you want me, when you know Jenna and I are friends, is…is incredibly selfish."

His chest heaved. "You think I'm selfish?"

"Yes!"

"No, *cara mia*," he said, his smile tight and bitter. "I have been a saint." His nostrils flared and his jaw hardened. "*This* is being selfish."

He stood so close, it didn't take much before his big hands had fastened on her arms and pulled her the few inches closer that allowed him to slap his mouth over hers. Senses shocked, Brenda froze, right before dizzying excitement careened through every single limb and she shuddered against his chest.

One hand lifted to her hair, cradling the back of her head as his tongue plowed into her mouth. The delicious intrusion dragged a thready moan from the depths of her throat, and her nipples beaded against the hardness of his chest.

The sounds of the night receded—idling cars, people talking, the hum of air conditioners. She breathed him in, lapping at his mouth with her tongue until his hold on her tightened to the brink of pain. Her fingers clutched the lapels of his jacket as he forced her against the wall and angled his head to consume her even more.

Brenda stroked her palms over his rough, hair lined jaw, moaning softly when the lean muscles of his belly pressed against the soft, convex surface of hers. He tasted even better than she remembered— rich and warm, almost exotic when combined with the distinct flavor of the wine they'd consumed.

Grasping fingers reached into his curls. Lost in the

thickness, they enthusiastically ran through his soft hair, stroking over his scalp until a shudder rippled down his frame.

Jay grabbed two handfuls of ass, squeezing and trying to tug her closer, as if that were even possible the way they were already wedged against each other. His mouth found the slender column of her throat and she tilted her head back. His breath was hot and heavy as he licked her skin, setting her body on fire and sending beats of heat to her clit.

He moved to the pulse at her throat, and her nipples tightened expectantly, wanting a touch, a lick, a graze, anything to show them some attention. The night sky loomed above with a spattering of stars, and the buildings swayed against the dizzying maneuvers of his mouth.

He whispered in Italian against her skin. He seldom spoke Italian, and why would he? She wouldn't understand. But this was beautiful, listening to the foreign words roll off his tongue. She may not understand, but she understood the intensity of emotions because she felt them, too.

She hadn't even felt him undo the top button of her blouse. Only aware it had been done because his teeth nipped the swell of her breast, and his moist tongue traced the line of her cleavage.

"Oh god," she panted, fingers tightening in his hair.

A groan erupted from deep in his chest. His body shifted and he planted a knee between her legs. That's when his bone stiff erection poked her in the belly.

The shock of his arousal penetrated the fog of lust and the reality of the situation sank in. They were on the side of a building in full view of passersby, exhibiting a glaring lack of decorum, tearing into each other with an appalling lack of decency.

Brenda pushed him away and wrenched free, breathing hard through her nose and mouth. They both were, staring each other down. The rawness of desire throbbed through her veins, her loins, her skin.

"I'm never safe with you, am I?"

"Do you want to be safe?" he challenged.

Her fingers touched her trembling mouth. "Don't touch me again," she said, in a voice not entirely steady.

He moved closer. "Brenda—"

"I said, don't touch me!" She retreated and ran her tongue over bruised lips. The delectable taste of him had saturated her mouth and would remain for days on end, again. "I've learned my lesson. Obviously we can't be alone together. Not even in public."

She turned and hurried toward the parking lot where her car was parked, rushing away from him as fast as she could.

Just like she'd done all those years ago.

CHAPTER EIGHT

She'd escaped. But what exactly had she escaped from?

Brenda sat parked in the driveway, elbows on the steering wheel, her head resting in her hands. Ridiculously close to tears, so upset and lost in her own emotions she didn't notice when Mrs. Chen parked beside her until the older woman rapped on the passenger window. Her head jolted up at the unexpected sound.

"Are you all right, dear?" The glass muffled her voice.

"I'm fine." Brenda assembled the most reassuring smile she could and exited the vehicle. "Long day, crazy day." Her fingers tightened around the keys, stopping the tremble that shook them.

Mrs. Chen searched her face, skepticism in her eyes, deducing she hadn't been completely truthful.

Brenda waved. "Good night." She went up the steps and paused outside her door, listening for her landlord's slow progress up the stairs. Once Mrs.

Chen safely entered the apartment above, she let herself into her own place.

The phone was ringing, and she hurried down the hall, past the two bedrooms and living room to the wide, open kitchen at the back of the house. She flicked on the light and reached for the phone but pulled back with the speed of someone who'd encountered a scorpion.

Jenna's number displayed on the caller I.D.

Not now. The timing couldn't be worse.

Her eyes remained fixated on the LCD screen until the shrill ring of the phone ended. When it did, she breathed a sigh of relief. But no sooner had she done that, the phone in her purse began to ring.

"Don't be Jenna."

Brenda set the purse on the dark walnut table and fished out the phone. Her heart sank. Sure enough, it was Jenna. Tugging her lower lip between her teeth, she gnawed gently and debated whether or not to ignore this call, too. At the last minute, she hit *Answer* before it rolled to voicemail.

She added an appropriate amount of excitement to her voice. "Hey, Jenna!"

"Hi, Brenda. Do you have a few minutes?"

"Sure." Brenda walked over to the kitchen cabinets and removed a container of tea, a fruity, fragrant blend of berries, grapes, and hibiscus.

"I told Jay about Dale."

Brenda had almost forgotten about Dale, but then she remembered their conversation from a while back. "You did? When?"

"Today." By the tone of Jenna's voice, the conversation must not have gone well. "I told him I wanted to introduce Dale to the boys."

Brenda filled an electric kettle with water. "How did he react?" She set the kettle on the burner and pushed the button for the tea setting.

"He didn't say much."

Brenda paused her movements, stomach muscles rigid with anxiety. "Did he...seem jealous?" She shouldn't have asked that question. Not when she feared the answer.

"We're past all that now, I guess you could say. I am, at least. I'd have to be, wouldn't I? The way he goes through women..."

"Is it hard for you?" Brenda asked, throat so tight the words barely came out. "Seeing him with someone else?"

Jenna didn't answer right away, as though she gave the question a lot of consideration. "Sometimes," she said slowly. "Especially..."

Brenda waited, a giant knot of dread in her stomach.

"Especially when I think about how we used to be." Jenna let out a low laugh, a quiet, knowing sound that hinted at intimacies and private moments.

Brenda reached up into the cabinet again, this time for a teacup and saucer. A pretty rose pattern adorned the circumference of each cup and the interior of the saucers. If she kept moving, she wouldn't dwell on the tone of Jenna's voice and could pretend her friend's admission didn't cause any distress.

"Our lovemaking was incredible. I hope this isn't TMI, but that's one of the things I really miss. He was amazing in bed. He gave it his all, you know? So...*intense*—"

The teacup and saucer clattered to the counter. With the phone tucked between her ear and shoulder,

Brenda scrambled to save the dishes from crashing to the floor. "Sorry about that," she muttered. She'd almost destroyed the dishes, a four-piece set passed down from her paternal grandmother.

"No problem." Jenna sighed. "Like I was saying, I miss the sex. Hmm. He really was a *stallion* in bed, and oh my—"

"I have to go." Brenda's words cut through, sharp and quick. If she listened to any more of Jenna's breathless praise, she'd be sick. "I have company."

Jenna gasped. "Oh my goodness, why didn't you say something?"

"I had just walked in when you called." At least that part was true.

"You finally found time in your schedule to start dating again? Yay! Call me tomorrow. I want to hear all the juicy details."

"We'll talk soon. Bye." Brenda hung up the phone and set it on the table beside her purse.

She then tore down the hallway to her bedroom and quickly stripped out of her clothes. They still oozed the spicy scent of Jay's skin and cologne. She tossed them into the hamper and went into the bathroom. In the shower, she scrubbed her body down with a soapy washcloth, twice, concentrating on the areas where her flesh had made contact with Jay—her neck, her arms, her breasts.

Afterward, Brenda dried off and rubbed scented lotion into her skin, threw on a robe, and padded back out to the kitchen. The kettle had kept the water warm so she still treated herself to a cup of tea. As an added indulgence, she opened a box of chocolate and pistachio biscotti and placed one on the saucer. The methodical motion of stirring honey into the warm liquid calmed her agitation to a quiet hum.

She entered the living room and sat on the Chesterfield couch, an old relic in deep chocolate that she'd picked up at a second hand furniture store for an incredibly low price. The other chairs in the room had also been steals. One, a leather recliner she'd found at a neighborhood yard sale, and the other a comfy camel-colored armchair with matching ottoman she'd bought at a furniture store's going out of business sale.

Shifting a beige and burgundy pillow out of the way, she settled in a corner of the couch and placed her heels on the edge of the wood coffee table.

She dipped the biscotti in the tea and took a bite of the soaked cookie. Tasty, but that wasn't the best part. When she sipped the tea, she tasted the fruity blend and the sweetness of the biscotti disbursed into it. Now she was better prepared to take a trip down memory lane.

She knew a little about the intensity Jenna had gushed about. She'd seen it tonight, but the first time she'd experienced it had been twelve years ago. She could barely remember what she'd had for lunch last week, but she remembered, in vivid detail, the first time Jay kissed her.

It had been raining hard, and since she didn't have a car at the time, Jay offered to drop her home on his way home. She'd readily accepted the offer because deep down, to her shame, she'd wanted that time with him. She'd spent half the car ride watching his lips when he spoke, not because she couldn't understand him, but because of the pleasure it gave her to examine the curves.

Her chest grew warm, and her nipples hardened

from the erotic memory of that night…

****

Jay pulled up outside Brenda's apartment building. Rain drenched the night in heavy sheets, but a couple of cars parked right in front of the door prevented him from pulling any closer.

"Darn," Brenda said, sighing. "Too bad we can't plough into their cars and make them move." She was trying to be funny, but Jay didn't laugh.

"That wouldn't be very nice to hit their cars," he said, in his heavily accented voice. She could listen to him read a grocery list. The *h* sounds dropped from his words, and his sentences lifted and danced at the end.

Brenda grinned at him. "I was kidding. You're such a good guy."

He stared straight ahead, his face oddly grim. "I'm not a good guy."

"Why do you say you're not a good guy?" she asked, mildly amused.

"Because I'm not."

She didn't know why he'd become so solemn or would make such a disparaging remark about himself. They'd had an interesting discussion on the drive to her apartment. He'd told her all about his home in Naples, his mother, and the close relationship with his grandfather.

In an effort to dispel the disturbing conversation, she stated the obvious. "It's really raining hard. I'll have to make a run for it."

Instead of popping the lock as she expected, Jay surprised her by pulling away from the building.

"What are you doing?" Brenda demanded.

He glided into a parking space farther away from

the front door. It was Saturday night and only a few cars were in the parking lot because many of the student residents were out partying one last time before they left for break.

Jay turned off the car and twisted in the seat to face her.

"What's going on?" she asked, her voice quiet, her heart pumping a little faster.

"I think about you all the time." He took her hand, and she let him. His was warm and comforting and made her skin tingle. "I don't know what to do about the way I feel. It is like…like a torture I cannot be free from."

His words shocked her. That he experienced even a modicum of the tumultuous sensations coursing through her every time she neared him, had never even occurred to her.

Her fingers curled against his palm. "Jenna's my friend." The statement was a reminder to herself and spoken aloud to set an obstruction between them. But it seemed he didn't hear her words.

His hand tightened around her fisted fingers and he slowly pried them open, one by one and with very little resistance. He planted a kiss in the middle of her palm. She should have pulled away, but didn't. Not even when his lips moved in gentle strokes to the inside of her wrist.

After that, everything happened so fast. He pulled her across his lap so that she straddled him on the seat. She'd never been in such close, intimate contact with Jay. Her pulse exploded with excitement.

He pressed his lips to her neck, and lithe fingers crept under her dress and between her legs. The warmth of his hand in her panties and the swipe of his thumb across her clit left her gasping and fueled a flood of sensations she'd never experienced before.

For a brief moment they paused and stared into each other's eyes at the realization of what they were doing. But all thoughts of stopping evaporated as he eased long fingers into her wetness.

She gripped his shoulders and pressed her mouth to his. Their tongues and lips tangled as she rode his hand. The pounding rain sheltered their act from prying eyes and composed a natural soundtrack to their furtive movements. Frantic, frenzied sounds filled the car.

Desperate to touch and satisfy her curiosity, her fingers popped the buttons on his shirt and she pressed her lips against his warm flesh. Groaning, he ran trembling fingers through the soft strands of her hair as she licked his chest and his nipples hardened under the stroke of her tongue.

His hand at her back held her close, and his mouth on her collarbone sucked the sensitive flesh there. Meanwhile his adroit fingers stroked and fondled, teased and rubbed, until she came all over his hand from an orgasm so impactful she gasped and tossed her head back.

Before she could even recover, the button on his jeans snapped open and he pushed down his boxers in an inelegant wiggle, enough to expose himself—long, hard, tumescent. And she was wet, swollen, and aching. For him. To feel him deep inside of her. The temptation was great. She'd never known such temptation, but she pushed at him, forcing as much distance as she possibly could while remaining on his lap. The steering wheel dug into her lower back.

"No," she whispered.

It didn't seem fair that she'd gotten off and now refused him when he was so ready. He looked into her eyes and stopped immediately. The stormy grey of his pleaded with her.

"Brenda, *tesoro mio. Per favore, ho bisogno di te.* Please. I need you." He cupped her face in his hands, but that single action was the biggest mistake he made.

She smelled the scent of her own musk on his fingers and pulled away. "I can't. *We* can't. No." She shook her head vigorously.

She climbed off his lap and, in a rush to escape to the other side of the vehicle, bumped her knee on the emergency break.

"Brenda." He reached for her and she knocked away his hand.

Scrambling for the door handle she stumbled out of the car, twisted her ankle, and fell onto one knee.

"Brenda, wait!" he called through the open door.

She pushed up from the ground almost as soon as she hit the rough pavement and ran as fast as she could toward the building. Rain battered her back, skin, and hair. Her knee stung where the skin had been scraped off in her fall, but she didn't hesitate to keep moving.

He called her name from a distance, sounding far away, but not far enough. She kept running and slammed into the door. Huffing, heart racing, she swiped her key card, rushed into the building, and ran to the elevator.

Behind her, she heard Jay pounding and the door rattling from the force of his heavy-handed shaking. She dashed into the elevator and hit the button for her floor. That's when she finally looked across the lobby at him.

He stood out there, his shirt still undone but pants zipped. A helpless, pleading expression filled those grey eyes. His hair was plastered to his scalp, and rain streamed down his face.

Her stomach clenched with guilt and regret. What they'd done was wrong. Sickened by her own behavior, Brenda averted her eyes.

Finally, thankfully, the elevator doors closed.

****

Brenda sipped the warm tea.

A week passed before she and Jay spoke privately about what had happened between them. They'd had a reasonable conversation where she told him they shouldn't have kissed or touched each other in that way. They'd made a mistake, she explained. She wasn't a boyfriend stealer and couldn't do that to her friend.

Jay didn't argue. He didn't fight. In fact, he had been very understanding and agreed they'd crossed the line. He even apologized, and they agreed to act like it never happened.

Yet every now and again when they were all together, she'd catch his eyes on her, and she hoped no one else noticed. Those looks lessened over time and dried up completely when a few months later, Jenna became pregnant, and she and Jay announced their engagement.

Brenda's feelings for him never completely died, however. After tonight, she could admit the truth. What she'd felt had merely been overlaid by life and circumstances. She'd learned to never get too close to him. To touch as rarely as possible. But those feelings remained.

And so for all these years, the rendezvous in the

car had remained their little secret.

CHAPTER NINE

Brenda locked her car and walked to the six-story office building where she worked in Alpharetta. Wearing a blue, pinstriped pantsuit and kitten heels, she shifted the Gucci purse into the crook of her arm and opened the glass door. She'd purchased the leather handbag used on eBay in mint condition, a present to herself for landing the job of her dreams, but the purchase had set her back a couple thousand dollars.

For years Atlanta had been touted as the "Hollywood of the South." Attractive tax incentives offered to movie-makers and production companies pulled the movers and shakers in the industry to the city. The *Entertainment Report*, or the *ER* as it was often called, set up a second office and recruited her from a smaller magazine in Chicago where she had been an associate editor covering lifestyle and entertainment.

More and more magazines were moving away from print. Many people read on their tablets and phones nowadays, so the *ER* was primarily digital, with only two special print editions every year.

"Who's the latest celebrity that you've met?" asked Dev, walking backward toward the door. A slender Indian man, he worked for an insurance company on the first floor. His clean-shaven face always wore a mischievous smile, a cross between a leer and boyish charm.

Brenda pressed the elevator button. "Yesterday I had lunch with Boris Kodjoe."

"Ugh." He placed a hand over his heart, feigning pain. "I don't stand a chance, do I?"

He was a terrible flirt, and she never took him seriously. Smiling, she said, "Dev, you know good and well it's me who doesn't stand a chance. Your mother would have a fit if you brought me home."

"I could make it work, Brenda. For you, I'd make it work."

"Uh-huh." She waved goodbye to him before entering the cabin.

On the way to her office, she stopped to chat with Nina, one of the interns. The young woman sat in the middle of the office at a table she shared with other interns.

"Miss Morrison, the concert was *amazing*," Nina gushed, placing emphasis on her favorite word. Her brown eyes were wide and as glossy as her raven-colored hair. No matter how many times Brenda said to call her Brenda, the young woman always used her more formal name.

As a perk of the job, she often received invitations or tickets to events. For events like a concert, such as the one Nina attended, she awarded those to interns who did a write-up with the help of one of the editors.

"So you enjoyed yourself?" Brenda asked, flipping through the mail.

"Yes. When we went backstage, it was incredible. They were so friendly and nice. It was *amazing*."

Brenda smiled. It was easy to become star struck in the entertainment business. Unfortunately, some interns thought the job was all glamour, but not Nina. She worked hard and did the grunt jobs nobody else wanted. That's why she was one of the few Brenda always thought of when passes became available.

"Glad to hear you had a good time." She tucked the correspondence she wanted under her arm. "Did you already send the writing clips?"

"Yes, ma'am. Already forwarded them to you."

Freelance workers who wanted to work for the *ER* sent writing samples by email with links to their articles online. Nina checked the designated email account and compiled the links into one email, which she forwarded to Brenda once a week.

Brenda greeted other members of the staff on the way back to her office, a glass room on three sides, but with a window and exposed brick on the fourth. Red and purple verbena in pots on the window ledge soaked up the sunshine and looked out onto a busy roadway. Their citrus scent welcomed her when she entered.

She set her purse on the polished wooden desk as Nina appeared in the doorway of her office.

"Have you ever listened to their music?" Nina asked, still talking about the concert.

Brenda sat down and crossed her legs. "No, but I understand it's very gritty."

"It is, but they speak for those who have no voice,

you know what I mean?"

The awe in her voice reminded Brenda of herself at that age—nineteen or twenty—before she understood celebrities were normal people, and before she knew she could have a job where she rubbed elbows with them on a regular basis. Stars who didn't get caught up in their own hype or press were often embarrassed by the adulation heaped on them.

"Yes, I know what you mean," she said. Unfortunately, she couldn't chat. "I have a meeting at ten. Would you order snacks from the cafe and make sure coffee and tea are set up in the conference room?"

"Yes. Sure will."

"Thanks."

Brenda scanned her itinerary for the day. Before the meeting she had time to check emails, many of which were junk, but she had to sort through them just the same. This afternoon's schedule was packed with more meetings and she had to review proofs of Ryan Seacrest's home and select which to use for the next installment of the segment on celebrity design tips. She was sending out replies to emails when the phone rang.

"Brenda Morrison," she said, mildly distracted by the words on the computer screen.

"Hi Bren."

Her ears perked up. Her mother, Samantha, only used the nickname when she wanted something. Samantha almost always wanted something.

"What's going on, Sam?" Years ago her mother had insisted Brenda and her sister call her by her first name. She'd had Brenda when she was young and thought it made her a cool, hip mother. She was always concerned about being cool and hip.

"Nothing. I just called to say hi."

"You never call to say hi."

"Well, I am this time."

"Tell me what's going on. You know I'm at work."

A heavy sigh came through the line, which meant Samantha had something potentially earth-shattering to tell her. "I'm getting married."

"*What?*"

"Calm down," Samantha said.

Brenda pulled in three deep breaths and rested her forehead against her fist. "Please tell me you're joking." What she really wanted to ask was, who in their right mind would marry an aging wannabe actress who regularly wore clothing inappropriate for her age? "Wait a minute, don't tell me it's…*him?*"

Samantha confirmed her fears. "Yes, it's him, and his name is Basil. Be happy for me, please. He's really a wonderful man."

Brenda lifted her head from her fist and twisted toward the window. She didn't want the employees to read her facial expressions through the glass walls. "You've only known him three months," she whispered fiercely. She hated sounding like a disapproving mother, but such was the nature of their relationship. Brenda was always the one to say *that's not appropriate, you can't do that,* or *have you no shame?*

Samantha had once been arrested for indecent exposure at the Caribbean Carnival in New York. Every year she flew to Florida for spring break even though she hadn't been on a college campus since she visited Georgia Tech during senior year in high school to 'see what the nerds were up to.' On a regular basis, random men in bars did Jell-O shots off her stomach, and she proudly proclaimed herself the reigning queen of the wet T-shirt contest, due to all the prize money and trophies she'd collected from sea to shining sea.

Perhaps even worse and much to Brenda's embarrassment, her mother had been the neighborhood MILF, rumored to have slept with several of the neighbors' husbands, and regularly flirted with the teenaged boys who practically lived in their house. No surprise, all the boys with raging hormones wanted to hang at the home where the mom flitted around in daisy dukes and fuck-me pumps.

"I've known him long enough," Samantha said.

"He's not even your type. He's over seventy years old."

"One day you'll be over seventy years old," her mother shot back.

"Yes, but I won't be engaged to a forty-nine-year-old!" *Breathe. Calm down.* If she didn't, her mother would clam up and disappear for a while.

"Forty-year-old," Samantha corrected.

"Whatever." Brenda rolled her eyes at the ridiculous idea that her mother was forty, which would mean she had Brenda at eight.

"Are you done? I called because I wanted to share my news, but you're being judgmental."

Brenda took a deep breath. "I'm worried about you. You're moving so fast, and this man—how do I know he's not going to take advantage of you?"

Too often her mother let hormones dictate her actions and was no stranger to men with slick conversations and bad intentions. The slickest of them all was Tracey's, Brenda's sister, father. Tracey was the product of an extramarital affair Samantha had with a movie producer who'd promised her diamonds and didn't even deliver a lump of coal.

"You're worried about him taking advantage of me, and his kids are worried that I'm taking advantage of him."

"You're not taking advantage of him." The very idea was ridiculous. Her mother's tasteless behavior demonstrated a glaring lack of maturity. She was naïve and didn't have a calculating bone in her body. "How dare they?"

"They'd probably say the same thing if they heard you," Samantha pointed out.

The somber tone of her voice gave Brenda pause. Had her mother only called to share her news, or did she also need a morale boost? If Basil's family questioned their relationship, she might be stressed and need support.

"I'm worried about you. But—I can't tell you what to do. Well, I can tell you, but that doesn't mean you'll listen." Samantha giggled and Brenda smiled at the sound. "Have you picked a date yet?"

"Not yet, but it'll probably be early next year."

At least they weren't rushing the wedding. Her shoulders sagged in relief. "I want to meet him. Promise me you won't get married until I meet him."

"I promise." Brenda heard the smile in her voice. "And I do want you to meet him, Bren. I didn't expect to fall in love, but he's everything I've been looking for. He makes me feel all warm and gooey inside, like chocolate chip cookies that just came out of the oven."

She'd inherited her love of sweets from her

mother. It was one of only a few things they had in common, because over the years she'd worked hard to be as unlike her mother as possible. As a young woman, she'd suffered from snide remarks that perhaps the apple didn't fall far from the tree, that maybe she had the same loose morals her mother did. She'd made an extra effort to stand out and apart from that type of behavior.

"I'll come to New York as soon as I can, even if it's only for the weekend."

"Take your time. Maybe I'll come see you, instead. Around the holidays, maybe? I'm not going to run off and get married without you. It wouldn't be the same if you weren't there, Bren."

Her throat constricted and her eyes became misty. Samantha sure knew how to get to her. "Damn straight."

"Do you think your sister would come to the wedding?" Samantha asked tentatively.

The relationship between her mother and sister had always been strained. Her sister didn't speak much to their mother. Like Brenda, she was often embarrassed by Samantha's behavior, but unlike Brenda, she didn't keep in touch. She'd gone to school all the way out in California and had as little to do with Samantha as possible.

"I don't know. We can ask."

"I would love to have both my girls there."

"I'll work on her, okay?" Brenda was always the peacemaker between them. "Now let me get back to work. I'll talk to you soon. Love you."

"Mwah. Love you, too."

Brenda hung up the phone slowly and stared at it for a few moments.

If Basil made her mother happy, did it matter that he had one foot in the grave and the other on a banana peel? Did it matter they barely knew each other? If they made each other happy, who was Brenda to judge or stand in their way?

CHAPTER TEN

She could get through the night. At least that's what Brenda told herself.

Freshly showered and clad in a terry cloth robe, she rummaged through the drawers of her dresser to find the right outfit. She hadn't seen Jay since after the wine bar. Nick was back in town and insisted they all get together before he flew home to Chicago. Fortunately, Sophie was also in town, and she would join them at the restaurant and promised not to bail at the last minute.

Brenda decided on an off-white long-sleeved blouse with an elastic waistband, cuffs, and neckline. The gauzy material made for a relaxed fit over snug-fitting jeans. She added a couple of bracelets and small earrings, and completed the look with a bejeweled forehead band.

Nick chose the Red Lion Restaurant and Bar, a newly open upscale establishment that boasted a lounge with low tables and white leather sofas. Located on the second floor of a building on

Peachtree Street, they offered a menu of contemporary American cuisine and California wines. She and Sophie ran into each other in the parking lot and searched for Jay and Nick inside.

"There they are," Sophie said, pointing.

Jay and Nick sat at the bar, but Brenda's eyes gravitated to Jay. He sat hunched over the bar, cradling a beverage and nodding at a comment Nick made.

"Damn, they look good, don't they?" Sophie said. "Especially Jay. We're lucky women tonight."

Brenda tossed her friend an annoyed glance. "You're in a relationship," she reminded Sophie.

Sophie arched a brow. "Doesn't mean I'm dead. I can look."

"You're only saying that because you're mad at Keith. Again."

Sophie shrugged, and they walked up to the men.

"Hello, fellas!" Sophie said with exuberance. She flung her arms around Jay first and gave him a kiss on the cheek.

Brenda glared at her friend. Her behavior was part of the bizarre relationship she had with Keith, which included outrageous flirting whenever they had an argument or took one of their "breaks." Right now, she was looking at Jay like he was the last piece of shrimp at a shrimp fest.

Nick grinned. "The ladies are finally here." He pulled Brenda into a hug and squeezed.

"Glad you made it back safely," she murmured.

When she withdrew from him, Jay's gaze flicked over her. "How are you, Brenda?"

No hug for her.

"Great, and you?" The other two were too busy

hugging and joking to notice the tension between them.

"I've been better," he said.

His face did look a little drawn, as if he hadn't been sleeping well.

"Let's go, let's go." Nick herded them toward the hostess stand with outstretched arms. "I'm ready to eat and find out what's been going on with all of you."

Jay pulled up the rear and bristled when he saw Nick place a hand to the lower part of Brenda's spine. He rolled his neck to relieve the tension.

"You look great," Nick said to her.

She did look great. Better than great, in fact. Her eyes had held uncertainty when she and Sophie walked up. She was unsure how to act, and he understood because he sure as hell was, too.

Nick and Brenda sat beside each other on one of the white leather couches in the lounge, and he and Sophie sat beside each other on the one across from them, separated by a square wooden table. It was almost as if they'd paired up.

He wished he hadn't come and hoped the time passed quickly, but no such luck. The evening dragged, during which he had the displeasure of watching Nick lean close and talk into Brenda's ear, as if it was so damn loud in there. The entire situation irked him, but he couldn't make himself leave.

For her part, Sophie mostly talked about her so-called boyfriend. Since she didn't ask Jay any questions, he faked his way through the conversation. Every so often he nodded and judiciously sprinkled noncommittal comments into the one-sided discussion so as not to let on he wasn't paying attention. But he wasn't.

Brenda had his attention, and he watched her from the corner of his eye, unable to keep his eyes off of her. Each time she laughed out loud gave him an excuse to look in her direction.

His gaze slid over her. Her hair was parted down the middle, long bangs framing her face. A forehead band sparkled with faux jewels against her deep brown skin. Even from several feet away, he could smell the sweetness of her perfume.

Nick openly flirted with her, and she was either too kind to rebuff him or enjoyed the attention. She chuckled at all his corny jokes and every now and again she'd touch his arm as she laughed. As if his joke was so…Fucking. Funny.

Jay ordered another drink.

"You alright?" Nick asked, eyes filled with amusement.

"I'm fine. Why?"

"You're really tossing back the Scotch tonight."

The comment took Jay by surprise. He didn't know Nick had been paying attention. He'd appeared so engrossed in the conversation with Brenda.

A tight smile pulled on his lips. "I'm a grown man and it's been a long week."

Nick lifted his hands. "Hey, I'm not giving you a hard time. It's only an observation."

Brenda glanced at him before busying herself with munching on a celery stick from the platter of fruit and vegetables on the table. They'd barely said two words to each other, and he was getting tired of her looking at him like that, with those big brown eyes that condemned and pleaded at the same time. Pleaded with him to stop wanting her and condemned him for how much he did.

"Sheesh, am I really that uninteresting?" Sophie asked quietly when Brenda and Nick were engrossed in yet another private conversation. Her gaze slid to Brenda and back to Jay. "Why don't you go for it?"

"Go for what?" Jay asked.

"Come on, Jay. You haven't taken your eyes off of her for more than two seconds all night, and a few minutes ago you had a look on your face like you wanted to kill Nick."

Jay frowned. "Don't exaggerate."

"I'm not. It's the truth."

"I was distracted. What did you say?"

Sophie rolled her eyes. "Nothing important." She took a sip of her strawberry margarita.

"You were talking about Keith, I'm sure."

She remained quiet and sucked harder on the straw.

"Now you want to go silent?"

Her eyes met his. "I know you don't approve. None of you do."

Her attachment to Keith baffled him. "Because you deserve better. Why do you put up with him?"

She didn't answer right away, stirring the red liquid in her glass with the straw. "Because he wants me." A bittersweet smile lifted the corners of her lips, and for the first time in a long time Jay paid close attention to Sophie.

"Plenty of men want you," he said.

"Not you."

He shot her a look that said *Stop, be serious.*

Sophie made a show of straightening the hem of her skirt and then crossed her legs. "He's the only one who keeps coming back," she said in a low voice.

Jay placed a hand on her shoulder and squeezed. She stared down into her glass. "Sophie, you're attractive, and you're funny. You have a lot to offer, and—"

"And there's a man out there who will see it. Blah, blah, blah. Yeah, yeah, I've heard it all before."

Jay let his hand fall and leaned close, elbows on knees. "There is, you know. But until then, life is short, and you're taking up all your time and space with Keith, which means you won't be open to the right man when he comes along. Take a permanent break from this guy. You don't have to settle."

Sophie's face tightened and her bottom lip trembled for a few seconds and then stopped. She bit her lip and cast a sidelong glance at him. "Since when did you become so sweet and nice?"

"I've always been sweet and nice," he said.

The sheen of tears filled her eyes. "You're not so bad, Jay."

It was his turn to share a bittersweet smile. "Thanks. I needed to hear that."

CHAPTER ELEVEN

By the time they were ready for dinner, Jay was in a better mood. Rather than sit at a table in the dining area, they stayed in the lounge and opted for the small plate choices. Eventually, the conversation turned to work-related topics.

Nick lounged on the sofa, one hand stretched along the back, which furthered the impression that he and Brenda were a couple.

Sophie dipped a fry in ketchup. "Brenda said DJ Terror will be at the Fulton County Community Center fundraiser. Isn't he one of your clients, Jay?" She popped the fry in her mouth.

"He is," Jay said shortly.

"Jay helped me secure DJ Terror for the fundraiser. I told you that," Brenda said.

"You know," Sophie said, stirring her drink with the straw, "you and Brenda should go to the event together. I mean, you'll both be there."

What the hell was she doing?

"I don't know what time I'll get to the center,"

Brenda said quickly.

"Neither do I," Jay added, voice taut. He was going to strangle Sophie.

Nick's gaze narrowed and bounced between Jay and Brenda.

"Well, you could coordinate your schedules," Sophie suggested. She licked salt from the glass. "The two of you are in complementary industries. You'll probably cross paths a lot, won't you?"

"Maybe," Brenda said. She set her plate on the table, having eaten only a corner of her cheeseburger slider.

"If they don't want to go together, stop pushing it," Nick said, laughing. He shifted in the chair, his face a little tight.

"I'm not pushing it," Sophie said. "It was a suggestion. What's the big deal?"

"It's not a big deal." Brenda arranged herself more comfortably in the chair. "But Jay probably has his own schedule with his staff, assuming he's even going. It'll be inconvenient for him to pick me up." She looked at him for agreement.

"In these modern times, maybe you should pick him up," Sophie quipped. She twirled a lock of hair around her finger. Oh, she was enjoying her little game.

Jay thought he should play along. What the hell. He didn't much care for how Brenda chose to speak for him and expected his ready agreement. "It's not inconvenient," he said. The look of surprise on her face filled him with a disturbing sense of satisfaction.

"I wouldn't want to—" she started.

"It's not a problem. In fact, it's a great idea. I'll pick you up. Let me know what time you plan to go to the fundraiser."

"I'll call you," she said. He knew better than to hold his breath and wait by the phone. He'd expire from lack of oxygen.

Nick cleared his throat and sat up. "Anybody talk to Jenna lately?"

They all looked at Jay and he tensed. "Not recently," he mumbled. The waitress arrives with a fresh glass of Scotch and set it before him. "The boys' birthday is coming up soon, so I'll be heading down to Florida to spend the weekend with them."

"How old are they now?" Nick asked.

"They'll be eleven in October."

Nick whistled. "Man, how time flies."

"It doesn't fly nearly as fast as it needs to," Jay said. He picked up his glass and welcomed the burn as he swallowed the drink.

****

Brenda was relieved when they finally exited the restaurant. They embraced each other and said goodbye. She and Jay exchanged a half-hearted hug before the valets arrived with her and Sophie's vehicles. They left the men, Sophie heading south, she heading east.

Nearing home, Brenda picked up the phone and dialed Sophie's number. She answered on the second ring.

"Hey, what's up? Miss me already?"

"Hardly," Brenda said. "Do you have time to talk?"

"Sure. What's going on? Something wrong?" The inflection in her voice went higher at the end.

"Nothing to panic about, but I...I need to tell you something."

"Okaaaay."

Brenda swallowed, apprehension in her stomach. "You have to promise not to tell anyone what I'm about to tell you."

"This sounds serious."

Brenda flicked the indicator to merge into the left lane between a truck and a sedan. "It is. Do you promise?"

"Of course."

She took a deep breath and blurted the words. "I have feelings for Jay."

"Jay who?"

"Jay."

"Our Jay? As in, Jacopo Santorini who we had drinks with tonight?"

Hearing her use his real name made Brenda laugh, especially since Sophie pronounced it incorrectly, as so many people did. That's why he preferred to be called Jay.

"It's Yah-koh-po," she said. "And yes, that's who I'm talking about."

"Back up. What am I missing? Where did this come from all of a sudden?"

"I'm about to tell you something, but it's complicated. I need to tell someone or I'll go nuts." Her fingers tightened on the steering wheel. "Jay and I had a—moment, I guess you could call it—years ago, when he and Jenna were dating. Over the course of our friendship, Jay and I developed feelings for each other. I don't even know how it happened— gradually, I suppose, but he was with her."

"Are you saying you and Jay…?"

"No, we never had sex."

"So what happened?"

Brenda decelerated and allowed a car to pull in front of her. "We kissed...and a little more than that." She wanted to bare her soul but wasn't ready to give all the details. "To further complicate things, I have a secret to tell you about me and Nick."

"Oh shit. What?"

"I had sex with Nick." She winced, waiting for the fallout.

"*What?* And you never told me?"

"It happened a long time ago." Brenda shifted in her seat, trying to get more comfortable with her confessions. It actually felt good to finally tell someone. "Nick and I had sex the night Jay and Jenna got married in Italy. It was a beautiful location and romantic and maybe I felt a little broken-hearted."

"You mean because of Jay? You had feelings for him way back then?" Sophie asked.

"A little." She sighed. "A lot. In fact, the reason I had sex with Nick was because of my feelings for Jay."

"You have to explain that."

Brenda thought for a moment. "When I first met Jay, I was attracted to him immediately. It was completely unexpected. But I convinced myself my attraction to him was no big deal and would eventually go away. Unfortunately, it never went away and only increased the more time I spent around him. Having those feelings had felt like a betrayal of my friendship with Jenna. Then one night, he confessed to having feelings for me, too, and he kissed me. We kissed each other."

"Wow. Where was I? Why didn't you tell me?"

"I couldn't tell you. I couldn't tell anyone. I felt awful because I enjoyed it so much, and because…you know…Jenna. Plus her father had gotten me that internship at his magazine. How could I betray my friend in that way?"

"So what happened afterward?" Sophie asked gently.

"We pretended it never happened, but of course I never forgot. Then the next thing I knew, he and Jenna were engaged. So…" Her voice trailed off as she recalled the pain of seeing her friend wave the large diamond under her nose. The jealousy she'd felt at the time had been almost unmanageable. "I know it's no excuse, but we were in Italy with wine flowing like water. And when Nick came to my room, he was funny and sweet, and we…I think we were both looking for something that night. We slept together the night of the wedding, after Jay and Jenna left for Paris. I regretted it the next morning, but Nick told me he loved me. I crushed his spirits and told him it was a mistake."

"Ouch."

"Believe me, the conversation was awful. He looked devastated."

"And then what?" Sophie prompted. "What finally happened?"

"He left my room. When we saw each other later, I asked him not to tell anyone. I don't know why it mattered, but I didn't want Jay to find out. Silly right? Considering he'd just married Jenna, and I was the maid of honor in the wedding. For about a month afterward, things were awkward between me and Nick. But he eventually called and we went to dinner. He insisted that he didn't mean to tell me he loved me. He'd gotten caught up in the wedding and the beautiful location."

"Did you believe him?"

Brenda thought for a moment. "No, but he'd wanted us to go back to the way our relationship had been before, and he'd promised he hadn't told anyone and wouldn't." She'd been relieved. "After the way he was behaving tonight, I'm pretty sure he still has feelings for me." Brenda pulled into the driveway next to Mrs. Chen's car but remained in her vehicle. "If I pursue a relationship with Jay—"

"Are you saying you want to?" Sophie asked. "Because I have to be honest, the tension between the two of you was noticeable tonight."

"You noticed?"

"Yeah. He definitely has feelings for you, too, Brenda."

She rested the back of her head against the seat. "This is purely hypothetical. If I pursue a relationship with Jay, then there are two people who could get hurt. Or at the very least, it would be an awkward situation."

"As far as Nick is concerned, he doesn't have dibs on your vagina because he had sex with you first. Besides, he's been married *three* times. Although, now it makes sense why none of his marriages lasted. Sounds like the first one, at least, was a rebound marriage, sort of an *I'll-show-you-I-don't-love-you marriage*, which ended in a disaster."

Nick's first marriage had lasted a little over two years before his wife filed for divorce, accusing him of mental anguish, among other damage. He'd been married two more times, and both marriages had also ended in divorce, though more amicably.

"Then there's Jenna," Sophie said thoughtfully.

"Her father's the reason I'm the entertainment

editor at the *ER*. He gave me an internship in college, and thanks to his connections, I landed the assistant editor job at the magazine in Chicago. None of that would have happened if Jenna hadn't spoken to her father on my behalf."

"If you owe anyone it's him, not her. But just like Nick doesn't have dibs on your vagina, Jenna doesn't get ownership of Jay's penis for the rest of his life. I've told you that before."

"It's not a good situation to be in, Sophie. If Jay and I get together, we could potentially hurt Nick *and* Jenna, and there's no doubt in my mind I'd lose their friendships. If a relationship with Jay doesn't work out, or if I tell him about me and Nick, I may lose him, too. And..." Her throat tightened. The nighttime darkness suddenly felt more oppressive. She'd already lost Jay to some degree but feared the finality that would come if he learned about her and Nick.

"*And,* that's the real issue, isn't it?" Sophie asked quietly.

Brenda didn't answer, but Sophie was right. She was afraid that if Jay found out about her and Nick, he wouldn't want to have anything to do with her.

"This is like one of those TV shows where all the characters have slept together at one point or another. Like "Friends" or one of those medical shows. I don't know the names, but I'm sure you know what I'm talking about." Sophie didn't have a television and thought it was a travesty to waste time watching shows which were, simply, time wasted in her opinion.

"Gee, thanks."

"Sorry." Sophie inhaled sharply. "Wait a minute, if

I'd hooked up with Jay, being that you like him, that would have been awkward."

"Yes, it would have been."

"You would have hated me," Sophie said.

"Probably. Now you see my dilemma."

Sophie laughed at her candor. "Oh sweetie, I know this isn't easy, but what are you gonna do? Not be happy because of some sense of loyalty toward Jenna? Or because of some sense of guilt toward Nick?"

Brenda gnawed her lip. "I don't know what to do, Sophie. Am I crazy? Am I overthinking this?"

"You can't always be the good guy. Sometimes you have to do the not-so-nice thing and think about yourself for a change. People do it every day."

"I'm not that person. I couldn't face myself in the mirror." Even now she felt numb and empty at the thought of hurting her friends.

"Tell me something, was it good with Jay?"

"Sophie!"

"Not in a sick, give-me-all-the-details kind of way, although you could if you want to." She snickered. "Let me rephrase. What I meant to say is, has anyone ever made you feel the way he does?"

Even before their first kiss—more than a kiss, as he'd pointed out—there had always been something between them. Their unmentionable secret had never been mentioned, but on rare occasions, he would look at her in a way that suggested he remembered, like she did. She'd had boyfriends and lovers, and after a time the rolling boil of passion had decreased to a slow simmer. But having Jay as a constant in her life all these years had ensured she never forgot.

"I've had good and bad relationships," Brenda said, "and I've been very happy in a couple of them."

"But has anyone ever made you feel the way that Jay does?"

There were plenty of eligible men in the world. Thousands. Millions. Surely she could find one as charismatic as Jay. The fact that she hadn't yet didn't mean he didn't exist.

Nonetheless, sadness filled her heart. She was torn, and she shook her head in answer even though Sophie couldn't see her. "No. No one's ever made me feel the way that Jay does."

CHAPTER TWELVE

Two other people received their vehicles before the valet arrived with Jay's Mercedes. When the valet pulled up with the SUV, both he and Nick hopped in.

"You okay, buddy?" Nick asked, putting on his seatbelt.

"Why do you ask?"

"You've been acting strange since I arrived yesterday."

"I'm good. *Perfetto*." Jay pulled out of the parking lot. Nick was staying at a hotel near the airport. Jay should have let Sophie drop him home to save himself the trip south.

"You don't sound good," Nick said.

"Well, I am."

They drove for several miles in complete silence. Nick fiddled with the air conditioner vent and moved around restlessly. Obviously he had something on his mind.

"What is it, Nick?"

"Am I that obvious?"

"Yes."

Nick glanced at Jay. "I'm crazy about her."

Jay's hands tightened on the steering wheel. "I guess you're talking about Brenda?"

"Yes."

Even though he'd guessed, the declaration still surprised him. "Are you serious?" he asked, to make sure.

Nick ran long fingers through his dark hair. "Yeah. I'm in love with her." He spoke in a forlorn voice and his expression was downright pitiful.

In love?

Jay opened his mouth to speak and then closed it. The collar on his shirt felt restrictive all of a sudden, and he unfastened the top button. "I had no idea you felt this way. Does Brenda know?"

Nick shook his head. Even in the darkness of the vehicle, Jay saw his face coloring in embarrassment. "She has no idea. If she knew, she'd probably cut all ties with me."

"Why do you say that?"

"You know Brenda. She's got a big heart. She would feel guilty and want me to move past my stupid crush, and she'd cut me off to make sure I did."

Jay silently agreed that sounded like something she'd do. Hell, she'd cut him off because of the way he felt about her, although the situation was a little different. "Don't you think you should maybe...do that, though? Get past it?"

A bitter laugh came from Nick. "Easier said than done. While I was in Europe, she and I talked every now and again."

"You called her?"

"To check on her, and to catch her up on what I

was doing. To be honest, it was completely selfish. The sound of her voice always brightened my day."

"You never told me you were calling her." Brenda had never told him either.

"It's no big deal, but it made having feelings for her harder to deal with. You have no idea how hard it's been for me."

Not true. He did have some idea, actually.

"She's everything I want, and I wonder if I didn't destroy any chance with her with all of my marriages." He ran a hand down his face. "At least when she lived in Chicago we could hang out. We'd get together for lunch or dinner or catch a show or something. Now that she's here, I'll never see her anymore."

In all honesty, Jay didn't know what to say to Nick's confession. He ran a hand over his jaw and let out a puff of air. "Tell you what, I'll come up to Chicago and we'll have a guys' night out. How's that? We'll party, get drunk, and screw a bunch of women."

That prescription had worked for him ten years ago after he and Jenna divorced. The more women he'd slept with, the better he'd felt about himself.

Nick remained silent and stared straight ahead. "I've already screwed a bunch of women. It hasn't helped."

"Listen—"

"I haven't been with as many women as you, of course, but lately, every time I'm with a woman, Brenda's face is the one I see. I have to face reality. I won't be happy until I can have her again. And I plan to convince her we should become a couple." He looked at Jay, determination in his eyes. Jay thought he saw challenge there, too.

"How are you going to do that?" A vein throbbed in the left corner of his head, threatening a massive headache.

"I don't know, but I'm going to do it," Nick said. "And I could use your help."

"*My* help? Whatever you have in mind, count me out."

"Don't you want to hear what I have to say first? I don't need you to do anything except keep an eye on her."

"Are you kidding me? No way," Jay said with vehemence. "No way I'm keeping tabs on Brenda for you."

"I'm not asking you to bug her phone," Nick said. He shifted to face Jay. "Just…let me know if she gets involved with anyone. If there's any competition. I can't keep an eye on her from Chicago."

Was Nick even listening to himself?

"You're out of your mind." He was going to forget this ridiculous conversation.

"Come on, man."

"You come on!" Jay ran shaky fingers through his hair. He was getting worked up, but he couldn't help himself. "I'm not your errand boy. We're friends, but I'm not comfortable keeping tabs on Brenda." Even if he didn't have feelings for her, spying on her—or whatever Nick wanted him to do—felt like a betrayal. Despite their frayed relationship, she was his friend, too.

"Great. You're the one person I thought I could trust with this." Nick crossed his arms and stared out the side window.

"I'm not going to tell her what you told me, if that's what you think."

"Fine. Forget I asked. It was stupid."

"We agree on something," Jay muttered. He heaved a heavy sigh.

They both fell quiet for a while. Jay pressed heavier on the accelerator. The sooner he dropped Nick at the hotel, the better, and they were almost there.

"Look, I was desperate when I asked you for that favor," Nick said, an edge to his voice, "but you're being a real prick right now. Don't tell me you didn't see the way she was touching me all night and laughing at my jokes. A good friend would help me out. A real friend."

"Or maybe you misread the signals," Jay said.

"You would say that," Nick mumbled.

Jay tossed a sidelong glance in his friend's direction. A definite sourness filled his tone. "What the hell is that supposed to mean?"

"You think you're the only one who women find attractive? The Italian Stallion, screwing everything that moves. You couldn't have Brenda, though, could you?"

Jay didn't like the direction the conversation had veered off in. "That would suggest that I wanted her." He pulled into the parking lot of the hotel and cruised to a stop outside the sliding glass doors.

"Don't pretend you didn't. Or that you still don't. It's so goddamn obvious a blind man could see it."

"What is so obvious?" Jay demanded. He slammed the truck in park and twisted to face Nick.

"You. You're obvious. The way you look at her. The way you drool. The way you undress her with your eyes. You were pissed tonight because she paid me more attention than you. You couldn't stand it.

You couldn't be happy for me."

"Your feelings for Brenda are clouding your judgment," Jay said quietly, between tight lips.

"I'm thinking quite clearly," Nick snapped. "You, on the other—it's not enough that you had Jenna, a woman who adored you. Or that Sophie finds you attractive. Or that every time we walk into a goddamn restaurant, the waitresses want to sit in your lap. You have to have the only woman that I've ever loved. Well, you can't have her, Jay. She's mine."

"Is she? Does Brenda know that?" Jay asked mockingly.

"Oh, she knows that very well. And she liked it."

What did that mean?

Suddenly, something Nick said earlier came back to Jay. At the time, it had sounded odd, but he hadn't paid close enough attention to break down why it didn't make sense at the time. Now the words came back in full force.

I won't be happy until I can have her again.

Again?

Jay stopped breathing, and one look at Nick's smug face told him everything he needed to know. But he still asked. "What did she like?"

"Let's just say she likes a man who can satisfy her. All. Night. Long."

"Are you telling me that you and Brenda…?" He couldn't bring himself to complete the thought, much less finish the sentence. The passage to his windpipe had narrowed.

"Fucked," Nick supplied.

Jay winced at the crude descriptor and the sheer pleasure Nick seemed to take in telling him. "How long has—has this been going on?" The headache attacked. It wasn't just his head that hurt, his entire being did.

"It happened a long time ago, but after tonight, I think there could very well be a repeat. Don't feel too bad. You can't win them all."

Jay fastened his hands on the steering wheel so he wouldn't put them around Nick's neck. He stared out the windshield. One of the bellhops was helping a couple load their bags onto a luggage carrier. Simple, orderly actions, while complete chaos expanded inside his head.

Brenda had slept with Nick. *His* Brenda had slept with *Nick*.

"Get out of my car."

"Don't be mad at her. She knows what she likes, that's all."

"Get out. Of my car."

"I'm sorry we kept it a secret from you," Nick said, not sounding sorry at all. "Brenda thought it best not to tell anyone, and I wanted to respect her wishes."

Jay turned to Nick, whose phony concern and insensitive remarks might result in bodily harm. "Get out. Of my fucking. Car."

Nick sneered at him. "I guess you're the one who misread the signals." With that parting shot, he climbed out and slammed the door.

Jay peeled out of the parking lot, his blood pumping fire through his veins. He ran a hand down his face, unable to fully comprehend what he'd just learned. She let Nick kiss, suck, and lick her, but she wouldn't let him touch her. His fist pounded the dashboard.

This bullshit couldn't be true. He wouldn't believe

a word until he talked to her.

Jay pressed harder on the gas, tearing up the highway toward Brenda's apartment.

CHAPTER THIRTEEN

Brenda's apartment and the one above it were dark. When Jay pulled in the driveway behind her car, the exterior lights came on and flooded the area.

He hopped out of the SUV and marched to the front door, rang the doorbell and waited. There was no movement inside the house, so he rang again, holding his thumb against the button for a long time. If she was asleep, goddammit, she better wake up.

A light came on somewhere inside. Within a few moments, the curtain over the window in the door was dragged aside and Brenda peered out at him. Her face asked the question, *What are you doing here?*

He braced his hands on the doorjambs on either side. "Open the door."

She opened it slowly, as if she wanted to keep him from entering. "I don't know why you're here at this hour, but it's late. I was already in bed." She pulled a lightweight robe tighter around her body. It was short, landing right above her knees. The impression of her full breasts was clear and obvious. He could even see her nipples. Nipples Nick had allegedly sucked.

He pushed past her and she closed the door, but they remained at the front of the house, the light from down the hall providing faint illumination.

His gaze drifted down to her breasts again. The little discs of her nipples protruded more prominently than before. Did she feel the tension between them, too? His groin ached and his fingers tingled with the need to touch her. He almost forgot the reason he'd driven over here in the middle of the night.

"Stop it," she whispered.

He lifted his eyes to hers. "You don't like it when I look at you?" he asked in a raw tone.

"It's inappropriate when you look at me like that."

"Is it inappropriate when Nick looks at you like that? Or do you like it when he does?"

She frowned, thrown because he'd mentioned Nick. "Why would you ask me—"

"Did you sleep with Nick?"

Her eyes widened with guilt. "What?"

"Did you sleep with Nick a long time ago?"

"How did you…how did you find out?"

"I give you credit for not bothering to lie." Jay took a few steps away from her and ran his fingers through his hair. "You won't even let me touch you. I hug you and you pull away like I have the plague. But you *slept* with Nick?"

"It just happened," she said in a small voice.

He rotated to face her again. "It just happened? When did this just happen?"

She licked her lips. "Didn't Nick tell you?"

"Oh yes, he told me. He took great pleasure in telling me, but he didn't say when." His neck drew taut under the strain of the unpalatable conversation.

"When doesn't matter."

His hands turned into frustrated fists at his sides. "It matters to *me*."

She stared down at the wooden floor. He heard the difficulty she had breathing. "The night you and Jenna got married."

The words cut through him. "*In Naples?*" He had no right to be upset, yet he felt she'd somehow betrayed him. He hadn't touched Jenna until they were on their honeymoon in Paris.

Brenda lifted her head. "You chose to get married there—*in Naples*," she said in a low, accusatory voice.

A tight pain seized his belly. Jenna had chosen the location, but true enough he'd gone along with the decision even though he hadn't really wanted to. Just like he'd asked her to marry him, when deep down he hadn't wanted to. A mistake he'd made in his early twenties in an effort to "do the right thing." And why not, when the woman he really wanted had told him to forget they'd even touched. As if that was possible.

The trip to Naples should have been under different circumstances. He should have been showing Brenda the city, allowing her to experience his culture, introducing *her* to family as his bride.

"You spent the night with him?" Envy seeped into his blood.

This time there was defiance in her eyes instead of self-ridicule. "Yes."

"How many times?" His voice shook.

"Stop it."

"How many times?"

She glared at him, like a cat about to attack and scratch his eyes out. "How many times what?" she snapped, even though she had to know exactly what he was asking.

"How many times did you fuck him?" he snarled.

"None of your business."

"Everything about you is my business," he raged. Why couldn't she have denied it? Then he wouldn't be consumed with envy. Then he wouldn't have this sick desire to know. "How many?"

"Your need to know is disgusting. It's beneath you." Her eyes flashed angrily. "But if you must know, not nearly as many times as you had sex with Jenna. Let's not forget that only months after you kissed me, you didn't waste any time getting her pregnant and then getting married."

"And immediately divorced."

"Why was that? She adored you."

"Adored me? A few months after the boys were born, she stopped letting me touch her."

"What?" Stunned disbelief crossed her face.

He didn't care anymore. Why keep this a secret?

"She withdrew from me. No affection, no nothing. She wouldn't even let me kiss her." The latter part of their marriage, he lived like a monk. He'd been tempted to stray, but the memory of his mother's soft sobs at night when his father had left her alone to go to his other women kept him in line. He didn't want to be that kind of man. "She was always too tired after taking care of the boys and the house all day. She said I couldn't possibly find her sexy or attractive anymore, and when I suggested we hire help, she accused me of thinking her incompetent."

One day they were sitting in the back of a hired car after dinner with her parents. As usual, they'd smiled and pretended all was well. She'd hung up with the babysitter and was smiling. It was so obvious she couldn't wait to see their sons, even though they were already fast asleep.

That's when he admitted the truth of their relationship. She used to be happy like that to see him. He wanted a little bit of that happiness extended in his direction, something to ease the dearth his life had become. Shamefully, he was jealous of his own kids and tired of being on the outside looking in. He'd reached for her hand right then, a last ditch effort to initiate intimacy between them, but she'd pulled back as if he was something disgusting. The hurt and embarrassment had been painful to accept, but even more so when she filed for divorce.

"What about all the other women since her?" Brenda asked.

The parade of women made him feel better, and he enjoyed sex. "And there haven't been other men in your life? Like the poor fool whose empty shell you left in Chicago?"

"You don't even know him."

"Yet I feel sorry for him."

"I didn't leave a shell. You make it sound as if—"

"You tear men apart?" he supplied. "You rip out their hearts and souls and their entire insides and then waltz away from the carcass? You did it to me. You did it to Nick, who you know damn well is in love with you, but you don't care."

She took a step back, eyes wide. "My god, is that what you think about me? That I'm some kind of monster who destroys men for sport?"

"Then explain your hesitation to sleep with me. Was it because you didn't want to be accused of fucking your way through all of us? Did you fuck

Charlie, too?"

Her lower lip trembled, but her glare could have sliced him in two. "You're despicable. You know I didn't."

"I don't know anything," he snarled. "I thought I knew you, but I don't."

"Are you listening to yourself? You and I were not a couple. You were already part of a couple, remember? But apparently that little detail doesn't matter to you. As far as you're concerned, it would have been fine for me to have sex with you, but sex with Nick somehow makes me a whore."

"I never called you a whore."

"You didn't have to. It's implied." She laughed, a high-pitched cackle, nothing like the cute giggles he'd grown accustomed to hearing leave her lips. He seethed in silence and watched as she covered her mouth and finally stopped laughing. "That's rich," she said.

"I'm glad you think this is funny. But I don't see the humor in the situation. You fucked Nick. Meanwhile you treat me like I'm a goddamn leper."

He ground his molars, angry at himself. Angry at what she had reduced him to—nothing more than a raging, jealous lunatic. A man who could have almost any woman he wanted, except her, the one woman he truly desired. The one who remained just out of reach.

"When I fucked Nick, as you so eloquently put it, you were a married man, so it was really none of your damn business who I was fucking. The only reason you're upset is because I didn't fuck you."

His hands clenched. He wanted to slam his fist into the wall. He stared at the door because he could no longer look at her. Not when looking at her meant thinking about Nick's filthy hands on her body, his mouth on her soft skin—licking, kissing. Doing what Jay wished for years he could do.

"Fuck all of Atlanta for all I care."

"Wonderful. I finally have your permission. I can sleep better tonight." She made glib comments while he was going out of his mind with wanting her.

Jay swung his gaze back to her face.

Maybe it was the defiant tilt to her head. Or maybe it was the way the thin robe enveloped her body and forced his halfway erect penis to become even harder as his eyes slid over her lush curves. *Something* pushed him over the edge, past the point of no return.

Jay charged across the hall and Brenda backed up against the wall. He caught her chin in his hand and forced her to look him in the eye. She grabbed his wrist and tried to yank away his hand, but he didn't budge.

"*Gesù*, why couldn't you stay in Chicago?" he rasped.

He slammed his mouth over hers and gathered her tight to his body. Her clenched fists pounded his shoulders, but he refused to let go. One hand ran up her side, over her ribcage to the opening of her robe. He pulled it aside and exposed a ripe breast. Full and supple, he caressed the soft skin and stroked the nipple until she moaned into his mouth. Her fists loosened and her fingers splayed wide, climbing up the back of his neck and into his hair.

He tore into her mouth, concentrating his hot, angry kisses on lips as sweet and perfect as a full-bodied wine. His tongue climbed into her moist mouth, met hers, and sparked a fire in his blood that had him fumbling for the belt on her robe. He released her long enough to see what his busy hands had revealed. Full, heavy globes with engorged, melanoid nipples. He groaned with satisfaction and dipped his head. He couldn't resist pulling a plump bud into his mouth. And she was so responsive, grabbing onto him, holding him in place as she arched her back.

Jay loved it. Loved hearing her moan, loved making her whimper, loved watching her tremble. He swiped a hand between her legs, but it wasn't enough to have his fingers down there. He wanted to gorge on her taste and fill his senses with her smell.

He lowered to his knees and came face to face with cotton panties. Peach-colored. So simple yet so sexy. He kissed the wet spot and ran his thumb over her covered clit, stroking back and forth over her swollen, damp crotch. She inhaled sharply and her fingers tracked into his hair. He sucked her through the cotton, merciless in his objective to provide satisfaction and get what he'd been denied.

Lifting her foot onto his shoulder, he splayed her leg wide and peeled back her underwear. Her body practically dripped with moist excitement, and he licked her shaved privates, dragging his teeth along the plump lips. Pulling her clit into his mouth, he sucked the turgid bud. She cried out and instinctively tried to jerk away, but his hands grabbed her ass, squeezing and keeping her glued to his mouth.

Damn, she was delicious. Tasty. Better than he imagined. This was what he'd been after. The minute Nick had taunted him, the minute he'd said he fucked her, a beast had been unleashed. A jealous beast that wanted a taste. A beast that had her pinned to the wall with a foot propped on his shoulder, wide open so he could sate his hunger with what he felt should have rightfully been his.

He ate and ate and ate, swirling his tongue in and around her aroused flesh. Calling forth an orgasm. Demanding a climax. Her head fell back against the wall, and her breathing fractured into laborious, irregular patterns.

"Jay," she wailed, as her fingers tightened in his hair, and tremors erupted deep within her thighs. He continued to lick, he continued to suck, until she let out a weeping cry, one that echoed in the empty hall and begged him not to stop.

The one leg she stood on shook uncontrollably. She pressed against his mouth, his head fastened to her body. He knew the moment the tremors turned into a full-on explosion. She gasped and rolled her head from side to side, every disjointed breath as encouraging as a round of applause. She pumped her hips against his mouth, clenching around his tongue.

Once again she cried out, a throaty, husky sound of undisguised pleasure, and her body went taut. She then whispered incoherently, shuddered in the aftermath, and slumped against the wall.

Nowhere near done, Jay stood upright. He wanted all of her. Everything.

With her eyelids at half-mast, her face held a drugged look, but they locked eyes. He removed her panties, dragging the cotton down to her ankles and kissing her smooth thighs on the way back up.

He unzipped his pants and shoved them and the boxer briefs to the floor.

Bracing his hands against the wall, he breathed words of outrage into her mouth. "Twelve years.

Twelve. Fucking. Years."

Jay lifted Brenda from the floor and impaled her on his engorged length, plunging deep.

"Oh god," she gasped, instinctively wrapping around him. "Jay. Jay."

The tremor in her voice spiked the temperature of his blood. His knees caved and he almost tumbled with her to the floor. But he found the strength to endure and pinned her against the wall.

Shoving deeper, he gripped her sweet ass and muttered a stream of Italian expletives. Dripping wet, warm, and tight, she felt incredible. He couldn't think in coherent sentences. Right then, he knew no other words.

He bit her neck. He licked her ear. He sucked her nipples. And all the while kept on pumping. Each powerful stroke bringing them closer to the brink, and her rotating hips a maddening, weakening agent of pleasure.

"I'm coming," she gasped, sounding surprised, as though she couldn't believe it was happening again so soon after the first.

He moaned her name into her shoulder, and when she screamed his loins erupted, shooting warm cum into her body. Winded and weak, he lost his footing then. Leveraged with a hand on the wall, he lowered his knees onto the hard floor.

She remained clamped around him, breathing heavily. His own breath tore from his chest in painful, loud huffs that made his chest rear up and down.

Slowly, her breathing regained normalcy and she lifted off of him. After gathering the edges of the robe to hide her nakedness, she knotted the belt.

Jay rose to his feet and pulled up his clothes. After

all the noise they'd made, the hall seemed oddly quiet.

"Satisfied now?" Brenda asked in an emotionless voice. Sadness filled her eyes. "Now you can go tell Nick you fucked me, too."

He regarded her in silence. Her eyes challenged him to deny what she thought to be the truth.

"That's not why I came," he finally said.

"No? You don't want bragging rights? You didn't come here for the sole purpose of getting what Nick got?" She crossed her arms. "You got it. Now you can check me off your list. You finally bagged me."

Shame heated his face. "I know what you're doing."

"Everything Jenna said was true. You really are amazing. You really are intense."

"You're held hostage by misguided guilt. There's absolutely no reason why two consenting adults—"

"You're so upset about me sleeping with Nick—"

"What now, Brenda?"

"I have a conscience. I have personal ethics. Do you?"

"So we pretend tonight never happened?" he asked, aghast.

She took a calming breath and stared down at the floor. "We were never a couple and look how you reacted when you found out about me and Nick. What do you think will happen if Jenna finds out about us?"

Dumbfounded, Jay stepped back into the wall. "Are you that worried about what other people think?" he asked in a low voice.

Brenda's eyes remained downcast. Deafening quiet filled the hall.

"I thought…" His voice trailed off on a harsh

laugh. If after the passion they'd shared she could still hold fast to the same absurd code of conduct that had kept them apart all these years, he wouldn't waste his breath. "I hope your conscience and your ethics keep you warm at night."

With the pain of rejection attacking every cell of his body, Jay walked out of the house and left her alone.

CHAPTER FOURTEEN

Red carpet events in Atlanta had the same glamour, pomp, and circumstance as star-crammed Hollywood extravaganzas. Covering the performing arts fundraiser for *The Entertainment Report* meant a night of work, but Brenda still had to dress with a certain amount of glamour to match the occasion.

For the evening, she went with a sleeker hairstyle, bangs swept away from her face, edges smoothed at the hairline with pomade and lifted higher on top than usual. The dress she chose was a strapless number. The bronze bodice sparkled and fitted to her waist before pooling out at the hips into a bronze and sapphire organza skirt.

Standing in the mirror, Brenda applied lipstick and spent extra time adding a liberal amount of makeup to her eyes. By the time her driver arrived, she felt pleased with her appearance, grabbed the matching shawl, and hurried out to meet him.

"It's going to rain," her driver said conversationally, looking skyward as he opened the door.

Brenda looked up, too. The sky held dark, ominous clouds that appeared even more so in the fading afternoon light.

"It will. I hope it doesn't rain too hard."

"Hopefully the storm won't hit until after the event."

She slid into the vehicle. "Let's keep our fingers crossed."

The performing arts center was awash in flashing bulbs and the usual TV correspondents as prominent community members and celebrities rolled up in their chauffeured cars and stepped out to be photographed by the press and onlookers. Brenda made her way down the line, took a few photos, and answered questions about the magazine. As a co-sponsor of the event, tonight was an opportunity to bring awareness to their publication and its impact on the local entertainment scene.

Inside, attendees floated around, talking and laughing with each other. She searched the open space for the photographers and writer assigned to cover the event. She spotted two of them in a corner with their heads together.

"Hey, how are you guys doing?" she asked.

Liza, the photographer, looked up from fiddling with her camera. "Great. I took some good shots of the arrivals."

"Is Bill here tonight?" Brenda asked. Bill was the other photographer.

They both nodded.

"He's still outside, and I'll get the candid shots in here," Liza explained.

"This is amazing," Lincoln said, looking around. "I

can't believe all the big names who came."

"Remember, we're not only interested in the celebrity perspective," Brenda said. "We want to hear from the community leaders. Make sure you get a quote from the lieutenant governor, and definitely seek out DJ Terror." She glanced at her watch. "He should be here in a few minutes and he promised us an exclusive. Do you have your press badge?"

Lincoln patted the spot over his heart. "Right here. I didn't forget it this time," he said with a sheepish grin.

Brenda gave him the thumbs up sign. "Perfect. I'll see you guys later. I'm going to circulate a bit."

She walked away toward one of the many buffet tables set up in the atrium. On the way, guests stopped her and expressed appreciation for the event, or in the case of several movie directors, they wanted to know how to get a write-up in the magazine. Each time she smiled graciously, chatted, and handed out cards that she pulled from her Gucci wristlet.

Finally, Brenda arrived at one of the hors d'oeuvres tables. The spread included a host of gourmet choices, but she had her eye on the shrimp and the finger sandwiches.

She paused midway through placing a shrimp and grits cake on her platter when a familiar scent invaded her nostrils. Jay. Few men smelled as good as he did. Or maybe she simply didn't notice. He'd come up beside her and looked spectacular.

Dashing in a black tux, dark hair coiled onto his forehead. His eyes slid over her dress, and her stomach fluttered.

"You look…" His mouth tightened, as if he'd reined himself in. Then a reckless gleam came into his eyes, and he boldly stated, "You look incredible. I watched you walk in and told myself I'd leave you alone, but here I am. I can't seem to stay away." He averted his eyes and muttered in Italian.

"Hello, Jay." Stay cool. Stay calm.

The corners of his mouth looked strained. He was about to speak when an excited female voice interrupted them.

"Jay Santorini, how are you!" An older woman opened her arms wide and gave him a big hug. "I've been telling everyone about you and the campaign Omega did for the children's hospital. Did you have a hand in tonight's event?"

"No, but we work with one of the entertainers who's performing tonight. Have you heard of DJ Terror?"

"Oh yes! He'll be doing the artistic performance later, am I correct?"

"That's correct."

Brenda swept a champagne flute from a passing server. She needed something to do with her hands. She half-listened to Jay and his gushing admirer and wasn't surprised when the woman pulled him away to speak to another woman a few feet away.

She tried not to let the heaviness of her heart affect her mood, but the coolness between them pained her. She'd lost him for good. They couldn't even be friends now.

She sipped her champagne and mingled with the rest of the guests, but her eyes followed Jay from person to person. He worked the room, smiling and shaking hands and exchanging business cards with potential clients. While no one openly ogled him, he definitely had a presence and attracted attention.

Women laughed hysterically at his jokes or batted their eyelashes or tugged his jacket sleeve while looking up at him through their lashes. She'd behaved similarly in the past, hadn't she? Stroked his arm, given him a playful shove.

Right now he was flanked by a songstress who'd flown in from New York and a documentary filmmaker. The singer was quite touchy-feeling, and the heat of jealousy rose in Brenda's neck.

Would he take her home tonight, or someone else?

She imagined him putting his mouth on some random woman. An actress or a donor's socialite daughter. Imagined him kissing or touching them intimately and getting that gravelly sound to his voice. She put a hand to her stomach. The thoughts made her nauseous.

Jay glanced in her direction right then. His eyes bored into hers as if he'd known that she watched him all along, and she shifted her gaze to the other side of the room, embarrassed she'd been caught staring.

"What do you think?" the man on her left asked.

Brenda swung her head in his direction. "I think…" Oh boy, she had no idea what he'd said. "I think you should send me your idea. Standing around here, I'll probably forget, but send me the details by email, and I'll see what we can do."

His face broke into an effusive, appreciative smile. "Thanks! I'll do that."

Before she could break away, a long time contributor to *Southern Art News* approached and pulled her into another conversation.

****

Jay set the empty glass of wine on a passing tray.

He'd been drinking in an effort to loosen up the knot of tension in his shoulders. In all honesty, it was more than a knot. It was a bona fide boulder. He could have sent someone else from Omega Advertising, but he'd come because he wanted to see Brenda, thought he could handle seeing her in a public setting. Not so. Every time he caught a glimpse of her, he remembered sucking her nipples, tasting between her legs, fucking her against the wall.

He wanted back inside of her. He wanted to be close to her, in her presence, in her space, laughing and talking and enjoying her company the way everyone else tonight could.

His gaze swept the large room. He'd lost sight of her when she was pulled away by Usher's publicist and hadn't seen her for at least fifteen minutes. Maybe that was a good thing.

****

Dinner was served with well-rehearsed precision. Afterward, the master of ceremonies introduced the sponsors and organizers, which meant Brenda had to go to the stage and say a few words. She kept her speech short but mentioned how proud she was of her involvement in the foundation's activities and looked forward to the additional programming and improvements that could be brought to the community with the money that had been raised.

After dinner, a band took over the stage, playing a mix of rock and slow ballads. She sat at a half-empty table with one of the Atlanta Falcons football players, who tried to get her number until she finally shot him down. He was now whispering in the ear of a young woman whose family owned a hotel chain headquartered in the city.

"Would you like to dance?"

Jay stood beside her chair, extending his hand toward her. She could say no, but that would be churlish and silly.

She took his hand, her fingers tingling as they touched, and let him lead her onto the dance floor. She stared at his broad back in the black tux and wished that things were different.

In the middle of the crowded dance floor, he pulled her into his arms. They drifted slowly to the cover of a popular song the band played. Three minutes in, his arm tightened around her waist and he pulled her closer. Her abdominal muscles answered by tightening. He was so hard and masculine. The scent of him pervaded her senses, and she actually felt weak in the knees, forced to hold onto him more tightly than she intended. In these heels she was only a few inches shorter, which meant she could easily turn her nose into his neck. He pulled her even closer, so close that anyone looking would have to question the nature of their relationship.

"You're a standout among all the women here." He whispered the words into her ear. The hairs of his beard brushed against her cheek, the same way they'd brushed the sensitive skin of her thighs, and his warm voice wreaked havoc with her sprinting heart.

"Jay…"

The fingers of his right hand were interwoven with the fingers of her left and tightened fractionally around hers. "I feel a little out of control," he said, laughing uneasily.

"We shouldn't…." Shouldn't what? She wasn't even sure what she wanted to say. She only knew that what was happening between them made her heart clench painfully.

He guided her in a slow turn, holding her inappropriately close. Her body pulsed and arched against his. The electricity generated between them could easily light the entire venue.

"Brenda." Again he spoke in her ear, but this time his voice sounded hoarse, pained, and tortured.

Then, as if he had a sudden moment of clarity, Jay pulled away. The sudden movement left her momentarily stunned, almost reeling. She could only stare at him as he shoved his hands in his pockets, leaving her empty-handed and deprived of his touch.

A bitter smile lifted the corners of his mouth. "You're right. We shouldn't." He looked around the room as if seeking an escape. "I shouldn't have even come here tonight."

Then he left her. Alone.

And more confused than she'd ever been in her life.

****

DJ Terror's painting performance was a success. While the band played an instrumental compilation of his most famous hits, the flamboyant former rapper created two original 40 x 60 pieces of art on stage. One, mostly in shades of black and gray, appeared to be the silhouette of a woman holding a child. The second showed the stark reality of growing up in an impoverished neighborhood in dark brooding colors of black, navy blue, and maroon. Both were auctioned off for hefty sums, and then the lights dimmed low and he did an impromptu performance that had the high-brow crowd on their feet, bouncing their shoulders and swinging their hips.

Brenda decided this would be a good time to leave.

After a few more instructions to the photographers and reporter, she went through a side door into the hall and had every intention of calling her driver when Jay came up behind her and caught her by the elbow. The warmth of his touch sent tingles scurrying up her arm.

"Heading home?" he asked, staring straight ahead as they walked.

"Yes. I'm done for the night."

"Did you drive?" He stopped and looked down at her.

She couldn't read the expression on his face and suspected he purposely kept his emotions hidden behind a veil of stoicism. "No, the magazine hired a driver for me." She moistened her lips with the tip of her tongue. "I was just about to call him."

"Call him. Tell him you have a ride home."

His jaw was set in such firm, rigid lines, it was clear he wouldn't take no for an answer. The heat in his eyes made her heart race.

"All right," she said softly.

CHAPTER FIFTEEN

It was raining. Hard. The storm that had threatened earlier in the evening lashed the SUV and filled the driveway with water.

Brenda visited the memories of another night when Jay had taken her home in the rain. The inner lining of her bodice chafed against hard nipples, and the panties she wore became a restrictive band that constantly rubbed against her clit and made her ache to tear them off.

She realized with a start that she'd sat too long in the truck and stared out at the rain. Fierce, heavy drops of water hit the glass and slid down the windshield in snakelike formations. A slight chill filled the air, and she gathered her shawl over her bare arms to heat her skin a little.

"Thank you for the lift. I appreciate it."

Jay's hands rested on the steering wheel in the two o'clock and ten o'clock positions, like someone learning how to drive. They tightened over the leather surface. "You're welcome. It was a great event."

"We raised a lot of money. We should have the final figures some time next week." She stared down at her hands. What else was there to say? Nothing, really. She was stalling. "Well, good night." She reached for the door.

"Wait. I'll come around."

Her heart gave a little jump.

Jay reached into the backseat and pulled out a black and white umbrella. Then he was getting out of the Mercedes, and she watched him round the front of it to stand on her side.

Taking a deep breath, Brenda opened the door and stepped out to stand close to him. The door slammed and his arm went around her, fitting her against his solid body so they could walk under the umbrella without getting wet. His hand was warm through her clothes, and she nestled against him, wanting to turn her face into his chest and breathe him in.

She resisted the urge and trotted alongside him as he hustled them to the front door. They bound up the steps and onto the porch with only a few droplets touching her hand and the hem of her skirt.

She fit the key into the lock and could feel the heat of his gaze on the back of her neck.

"It's raining really hard," he said. "Mind if I come in for a cup of coffee or tea while I wait out the storm?"

Unable to determine his mood by the neutral tone of his voice, she turned to him, but the exterior lights backlit his head and cast his face in shadow, making it hard to read his expression. "Sure. That's not a problem."

He closed the umbrella and set it against the outer wall.

Brenda opened the door and flipped the light switch, illuminating the hallway. The house was oppressively quiet tonight, or maybe only seemed that way because she and Jay were quiet as they walked, past the living room and the open door of her bedroom. They didn't laugh or talk.

In the kitchen, she set her wristlet and shawl on the counter and kicked off her heels.

"Tea or coffee?"

"Tea."

She opened the cabinet door. "Black? Green?"

"You decide," he replied.

She filled the electric kettle with water and plugged it in. While the water warmed, she reached up into the cupboard and pulled down two of her grandmother's cups with the matching saucers.

"Sugar or honey?"

She turned around and caught him staring at her ass. She swallowed hard to quell the violent lurch of her stomach. He didn't blush or appear the least bit embarrassed. He just stood there, with his hands turned backward and gripping the heavy walnut table behind him.

"Honey." His voice was definitely lower, guttural, and goose bumps popped up on her arms.

Brenda went through the motions of preparing the tea. She placed a honey packet and teaspoon on a saucer. Dropped a teabag into the cup. Poured hot water over it. Then taking a deep breath, she walked over to him. The cup rattled against the saucer in her unsteady hand.

"This was my grandmother's tea set," she said.

Jay took the dishes and set them on the table. Before she could walk away, he grasped her wrist and held her in place. "I don't care about tea or dishes, Brenda. That's not why I'm here. That's not why you allowed me to come in."

Her eyes ran down his features, and he moved closer. So close that when she looked at him, she saw the short lashes on his lower lids.

"You let me in because you know what I want. And I know what you want."

"What do you think I want?" she asked, a slight tremor in her voice.

"I *know* you want me. Like I want you. I want to lose myself inside of you again."

Her lips went dry, and she moistened them with her tongue. He followed the movement with his eyes and continued to stare at her mouth when he asked in a low, hot voice, "Was that an invitation?"

In lieu of waiting for an answer, he jumped to his own conclusions and dipped his head. His kiss was soft, yet firm, and she moaned a little, shivering at the magnitude of excitement that filled her. He applied the right amount of pressure and there was the right amount of moisture in his kiss. The need for him was so strong, she shook from the force of it.

He pulled at the fullness of her bottom lip with his teeth, a playful tug that only served to arouse her more. She leaned into him, craving a closer connection.

His hands cupped her face and held her head in place as he deepened the kiss. He plied the seam of her lips with his tongue until it opened for him. Then he dipped in and their tongues touched. They both moaned at the contact and he forced her mouth wide, one hand tightening on the back of her head. Lordy, he tasted good.

The faint aroma of his cologne filled her nose, but more than anything, his individual scent—a scent she'd become acutely aware of over the years. She gripped his tight forearms when she threatened to sway on her feet.

Sensing her need to maintain balance, Jay switched positions and nudged her to the table until her bottom hit the edge. Over and over he continued a relentless sweep of her mouth with his tongue, stroking every corner, tasting every nook. His kisses left her out of breath and coaxed purrs from her chest.

She raised onto the tips of her toes and rubbed against the hard ridge of his erection, seeking relief from the pulsing ache between her legs. His hips pushed back and she gasped with pleasure. The intimate contact only deepened and tightened the coil of hunger that roiled in her abdomen.

Jay lifted his head and the moist sound of separation whispered between them. His grey eyes locked with her half-closed brown ones.

He breathed hard. The wall of his chest moved up and down in rapid succession. "If you don't want to do this, if you want me to stop, you have to tell me now." His already deep voice had fallen lower under the strain of need.

"I don't," she said in a shaky voice. But right away she saw he misunderstood what she meant because his eyes dulled. Her fingers tightened around his arm. "No, I mean I don't want you to stop."

Passion flared in his eyes, and when he kissed her again, she ceased thinking. His kiss was harder and held more intent. One arm wrapped around her body and his hand dragged up her dress. He stroked her thigh and ran his hand over her hip.

Then, without warning, he lifted her onto the table.

Gripping his firm deltoids, she hauled him closer. His kisses covered her neck even as his hands maneuvered the zipper at her back, and he pulled the bodice down, exposing her breasts to his heated gaze. He lowered her onto the table, the hard surface at her back as he brought his mouth down and sucked a breast.

"Mmm." She arched into the tugging motion. The sensations of his warm, moist mouth made her ache to be filled.

His pink tongue flicked over the dark tips of her breasts and she bit down on her lip, heat flaring in her belly as he moved from one to the other. He savored them, using vigorous sucking and thorough strokes that left moisture on the areolas and each swollen nipple.

In a rush, he cast aside his jacket and undid his pants. While outside, thunder crashed. A reminder that a storm powerful like the one in the kitchen raged outdoors.

She started to remove her thong, heart racing at the unveiled desire in his eyes as he watched her wiggle free.

"Let me," he said, his voice strained, his face taut.

Blunt fingertips dragged against her heated skin as he hurried her thong down her legs and tossed it aside. When he'd removed the piece of silk, he lifted one leg and kissed behind her knee, down to her calf, and around her ankle. His tender kisses made her ache even more. She wanted him so much. She wanted him on top of her. She wanted him *inside* of her. Gathering the full skirt of her dress, she hauled the material up past her hips and exposed her nakedness to his full view.

Breathing labored, his eyes remained riveted between her legs, as if he couldn't decide what to do next. Then his jaw tightened, and with nostrils flaring, he dropped his pants. He had barely lifted both her legs before he fed his body into hers with utmost urgency. Knees pushed back into her chest, she cried out, full and stretched. His hands gripped her hips, bruising the tender skin as he plunged into the wet sheath of her body. His face transformed into a heated mask of lust, and his lips parted on each ragged, exhalation of breath. The rawness of uncensored emotion in his face sent her heart tripping against her breastbone and heightened the arousal that dominated every molecule of her body.

Even with her limited mobility, they moved together, perfectly in tune, pumping faster. The table protested and the wooden feet squeaked across the surface of the tile with each significant movement.

The kitchen lights flickered from the raging storm, but that didn't stop them. It didn't slow them down. If anything, it made their actions even more frenzied. Covering her throat and shoulders in kisses, he was careful not to overlook a single inch of skin.

The pouring rain swathed the room in dull light and noise from its heavy drops. Lightning flashed as the teacup fell to the floor and shattered. Brenda didn't even acknowledge the crash. She didn't dare, refused to even slow down lest Jay stopped. Instead, her fingers climbed into the loose curls of his hair.

He pumped his hips with such concentrated intensity, all she could do was yield to the power of each thrust and raise her hips with the same level of urgency.

Sharp cries of pleasure ripped from her throat. She arched her body into the strength of his. The flat surface gave no comfort to her back, but she couldn't care less. All she wanted was more and more of Jay.

He thrust faster and faster, fucking her like his life depended on it, fucking her like he wanted to climb inside her body. They didn't stop until the explosion of stars behind their eyes signaled the climactic end to their wild, out of control tryst.

****

Brenda sat on the table, holding her bodice up under her arms as best she could because she couldn't reach the back to zip her dress. Jay zipped his pants but left the wrinkled shirt tails out. His hair was sticking up in several spots from the work of her busy fingers.

He appeared totally unkempt, yet sexy and masculine at the same time. It almost pained her to look at him because she wanted him again with such an acute level of need.

Her eyes darted to, and then quickly away from, her thong crumpled against the baseboard in the corner. The spilled tea had sprayed the bottom of two of the cabinets, and shards of glass lay scattered across the tile.

Jay cleared his throat. "I—"

"Don't say you're sorry," she said quickly. "Because I'm not."

His eyes remained on her, contemplating, assessing. "How do you feel?"

She ducked her head and rearranged the skirt of her dress. "I'm not sure, but it was almost inevitable, don't you think?" They no longer had the wherewithal to resist the potent attraction between them.

"Yes."

She lifted her eyes. She wanted to see his expression when she said the next words. "You're Jenna's ex-husband."

A muscle in his jaw flexed. "That should have been enough to stop me, but it didn't."

"It didn't stop me, either." She made a failed attempt at a smile. Instead, her upper lip trembled. "Obviously what we did was spur-of-the-moment."

"Obviously."

Brenda smoothed the wrinkles in her skirt, her eyes pinned to the plush fabric. "Staying away from each other hasn't worked very well," she said in a low voice. The rain was still coming down and the sounds created a solemn backdrop to her words.

He didn't respond, and she looked up at him again. The determination in his eyes was a response even before he spoke. "I can't stay away from you anymore." His jaw tightened. "I can't do another twelve years." His voice lowered as he came nearer. His eyes transfixed her, and they were so close she felt his breath on her face when he spoke. "I can't do another year. I can't do another month, I can't do another *day* without you."

He kissed her again. Moist, soft kisses, and she kissed him back.

"*Ho bisogno di te*," he said against her mouth, looking down at her through heavy-lidded eyes. "*Ti desidero*."

Her top fell away and he lifted one hand to cup her naked breast. He dropped a kiss on the soft skin.

Then he picked her up from the table with great care. She tightened her arms around his neck and stared into his grey eyes. The pupils were dilated and the irises dark and stormy with desire.

"Bedroom," he said.

Brenda nodded. "Yes. Yes," she said in a shaky, breathless whisper. She needed more of him, all of him, knowing that she'd never be satisfied with anything less.

He covered her mouth again and strode with her in his arms to the bedroom.

Chapter Sixteen

The kind of loving they'd shared made Jay not want to move, not want to do anything but stay wrapped around her, their naked bodies spooning. To just lay here and smell her and bask in the fact that she was finally his at last.

Dawn hadn't broken yet, but it was coming soon enough, and he wondered how Brenda would react when she had to face what they'd done in the daylight.

In the room's ambient light, he examined her in detail—what he'd wanted to do for years. He pulled gently at the curls at the back of her neck. Soft, like her skin.

His blunt fingertips traced the line of her spinal cord. The terrain of her back was a mixture of browns—deep amaretto at the top that faded to a patch of medium brown above her bottom.

Two flat moles on the right below her shoulder blade drew his lips. He pressed kisses there and let his tongue savor the salty goodness of her skin.

Brenda came awake with languid stretches. As she moved, his hand slid over her hip and down to her thigh. He felt himself getting hard at the prospect of early morning sex.

"Do you regret it?" he murmured into her neck.

She didn't answer right away, and he thought she wouldn't answer at all.

Then, quietly, "No."

He breathed easier and contented himself with nibbling the shell of her ear.

"We have to tell Jenna, and we have to tell Nick."

At the mention of Nick, Jay bristled, recalling how Nick had rubbed their night together in his face.

"Nick will be devastated," she said.

Not that Jay gave a shit. "You're exaggerating," he said against her shoulder. He rubbed his hand over her soft belly. Now that he had permission to touch her at will, he might never stop.

Brenda looked back at him. "I'm not."

She rolled over onto her back, offering him a nice view with the colorful sheet twisted around her waist. Her breasts weren't particularly large, but they were lovely to look at. Brown and smooth, with large, almost black nipples jutting up at him because she was partially aroused. He didn't think he'd ever seen her more appealing than in that moment. It was probably his male ego, but with the tousled hair and the passion mark on her neck, she looked like a woman who had been ravished all night. Mentally he patted himself on the back. He'd been the lucky bastard who'd had the good fortune to do the ravishing.

He kissed the tip of each breast.

"Jay." A finger under his chin lifted his gaze to

hers. Her voice had been firm, but she was smiling. "He's always been a little jealous of you."

She pulled the sheet up over her breasts and he dragged it back down.

He frowned. "Why do you say that?"

"Some comments he's made a few times make me think so. I thought it was in the past, but I don't think so anymore."

"We've had friendly male competition, yes, but...it's not what you're suggesting. It's a man thing."

"No, it's not." He could see her wrestling with the decision to share more. She gnawed the corner of her mouth. "He thinks you've lived an easy, maybe even a charmed life, because of your family's wealth and...you know, all the women you've slept with."

He reared back on an elbow to get a good look at her. "Are you saying you don't want to tell him? I want to continue seeing you, Brenda. You and *only* you." He had to make that clear.

"In all the years I've known you, you've only been in one serious relationship, and that was with Jenna. I don't have any expectations." She swallowed, a clear indication that she said what she thought he wanted to hear.

"I *do* have expectations. You're different. You're the one I want," he said. The Italian Stallion comments had gone unchecked for years, but none of those women held a candle to Brenda. For her, he was ready to burn his player card.

Doubt surfaced in her eyes, but she offered a timid smile. "Okay, we can see where this goes—for now. But let's keep it between us first, okay? Everyone doesn't have to know, and Nick doesn't even live here. He's in Chicago."

"We have mutual friends," Jay pointed out. "I'm not sneaking around like a criminal. We're not doing anything wrong."

"I'm asking for a little time so I can tell him in my own way."

"*We'll* tell him."

"Okay."

She didn't look convinced, and he didn't see the point in pushing. Their togetherness was too new.

He took her hand and kissed the knuckles. "This was unexpected for me, too. Us, everything. But we have nothing to feel guilty about. Okay?" He stroked her soft cheek.

"Okay."

They would continue to see each other. Any other course of action didn't make sense. Not when there was so much passion between them, and not when they knew each other so well.

They agreed Jenna would have to be told first, so even Sophie couldn't know yet. Jay suggested they wait until after the boys' birthday party in October. He wanted to tell his ex-wife in person, and he'd do it when he traveled to Bradenton.

"Now how about some morning sex," he murmured.

She giggled and opened her legs to welcome him.

****

They spent the next couple of weeks before the trip getting the property in Grant Park ready for sale. Jay donated most of the furniture to charity but saved a few pieces for the house in Alpharetta. It was his year to have the boys for the holidays, and he planned to have the house decorated in time for Christmas.

With the help of Brenda and an interior designer, he selected homey, comfortable furniture for the dining room and great room.

The designer found a bedroom set at a high-end store in Midtown that they both loved. With the three rooms he'd use most often ready, Jay moved into the new house.

The night before he went to Bradenton, he and Brenda were both at the house. Jay reclined on the sofa and Brenda prepped dinner in the kitchen. His house already felt like a home with her spending so much time there.

He watched her come into the room. She wore tight-fitting jeans and a green cashmere sweater. She'd been quiet ever since she arrived, and Jay knew she worried about the weekend's outcome after he told Jenna about their relationship.

He opened his arms. "Come here."

She came to him and settled against his chest. She fit perfectly against his ribs, like she'd belonged there all along. He brushed her bangs from her face and kissed her forehead. Gently, he rubbed her back. "It'll be fine," he said.

"I'm glad you think so. After everything Jenna's done for me…"

"You don't owe her for the rest of your life," he chided.

"She spoke to her father on my behalf, and he opened doors for me. I wouldn't have this job today if it weren't for the doors he opened. No one would have hired me as an assistant editor straight out of college. I had no experience."

"Her father may have arranged an interview at the magazine in Chicago, but you impressed them in the interview. That's why they hired you. And now you're the entertainment editor for the *ER*. That's all you— earned on your own merits."

"Yeah." She didn't sound convinced.

He knew she had other concerns. Mostly that somehow her behavior would be seen as improper, similar to the way her mother often behaved.

"What's the alternative?" he asked gently, stroking her hair. "That we sneak around? Or would you prefer that we stay away from each other for another twelve years? I don't know about you, but I can't live in that kind of torture again. Certainly not now. Not when I know what true happiness is."

She lifted her head, and her expression softened. "You're right, of course. Now that I know real happiness, I don't want anything less, either." She touched his cheek. "Are you sure you don't want me to come, too?"

"I think having you there would make the situation worst. She'd think you were coming there to spend time with her, and then we'd blindside her with our relationship. It's better this way."

She nodded and looked thoughtful for a while. "Have you heard from Nick?"

"No, have you?"

"Once. He admitted he told you about the night in Italy and apologized. We only talked for a few minutes, and I haven't heard from him since then."

She rested her head on his chest again.

Nick would be next on the list, but for now, Jay wouldn't worry about him.

CHAPTER SEVENTEEN

"Thank you."

Jay took the keys from the rental car agent at the Bradenton airport and found the Chrysler SUV in the parking lot. After stowing his bag and the gifts in the vehicle, he drove to the Holiday Inn where he'd stay for the next two days. It was several steps down from his usual travel accommodations but located close to his ex-wife's home.

Jenna had grown up in Bradenton, a small city south of Tampa. During their relationship, whenever they'd had problems, she returned to this familiar territory where she had family and a small pocket of friends.

He called her from the hotel.

"Hi, Jay." She already sounded tired from the amount of preparation involved with the boys' celebration.

"I'm here," Jay said, dropping his bag on the end of the bed. "The boys around?"

She called his sons and they came on the phone

with excited voices. "Hey, Dad! You coming soon?" Marco asked.

"Where are you?" Arturo added.

Jay grinned, looking forward to the coming celebration and spending the next couple of days with his sons. "I'm at the hotel in Bradenton. I'll be there in a little bit," he promised.

Their excitement made him excited, too. He never took the bond with his sons for granted.

His marriage to Jenna may not have lasted, but he gave her credit for being an excellent mother. She seldom asked for anything and kept the boys grounded. The house he'd bought for them was a modest four-bedroom in a quiet neighborhood of middle-class residents, much lower on the economic scale than he could afford. But with the beach a short bike ride away and cousins aplenty in the same city, the boys always appeared happy, and for that he was grateful. He hoped when they moved to Atlanta they'd be equally content.

Less than an hour later, Jay parked on the street outside the nondescript-looking brick ranch. He stepped out of the car and surveyed the property. A big "Happy Birthday" sign adorned the door, and colorful balloons framed the top and sides. Before he even made it up the walkway, the door flew open and Arturo yelled over his shoulder, "He's here!" before bolting across the lawn. Marco came rushing out behind him, and soon he was almost knocked to the ground as both boys flung their arms around him.

"Happy birthday, boys," Jay said, grinning and wrapping his arms around their smaller bodies. He dropped kisses on top of their heads and patted their backs. "You having a good one so far?"

"Better now you're here," Marco said, looking up at him with a toothy grin.

Jay ruffled his blonde hair. "I'm better now that I'm here, too." The hardest part of the divorce had been the lack of daily contact with his children. Summers and holidays were insufficient, and their Alpharetta move-in date couldn't come fast enough. "Help me get your gifts from the car."

The boys raced toward the rental—always running, those two—and retrieved the boxes from the back seat. Then the three of them walked to the front door, and he listened as they recounted their adventures for the day with their cousins, who had already arrived.

The birthday party attendees included the boys, Jenna, her widower brother and his three young children, Jenna's mother Martha, and friends of the boys'. Their friends weren't due for another hour, but the festive decorations were already on full display.

Streamers covered the entrance into the dining room, decorated with more balloons and party favors in blue, green, and white. Leading to the backdoor was a stockpile of neon water guns that glowed in the dark, for the nighttime "war" the boys had planned later.

"Dad, want to play the game with us?" Arturo asked. Their three cousins were sprawled on the floor in front of the television. On the screen, animated military figures crawled through the jungle with bullets flying overhead.

"Maybe later. I'm going to find your mother."

"She's in the kitchen with grandma," Marco said, plopping down on the carpet.

The smell of food guided him toward the kitchen.

Jenna had learned to cook authentic Italian meals, and his mother had even shared a few recipes with her. He already knew today's menu: spaghetti and meatballs and shrimp alfredo, with heaping salads and plenty of artisan bread. If they were lucky, which he was certain they were, his former mother-in-law had baked a 7-up cake to go with the gelato Jenna had bought.

Almost to the kitchen, Jay ran into Dale and pulled up short. His presence at the party came as a surprise. Right away, he remembered him from their wedding.

He extended his hand and Dale took it. "How's it going?"

Dale's hand grasped his. Clammy, probably from nerves.

Jay sized him up. He was shorter by a few inches and stocky. He'd aged somewhat, but they all had.

"Good to see you again," Dale said. He laughed, a nervous titter that manifested as a grimace.

To put him at ease, Jay fixed his face into an easygoing smile. This wasn't a pissing contest, at least as far as he was concerned. "Good to see you. It's been a long time."

"Sure has." Dale rubbed his hands together and took a deep breath. "Listen, I wondered if we could talk privately for a few minutes. Man to man."

"Sure." Jay found the words *man to man* a little amusing, but he respected the guy for getting straight to the point. He followed Dale out to the back porch.

Dale ran his fingers through his blonde hair and smiled a little uneasily. "Look, I wanted you to know that I have no intention of trying to get in between you and the boys. I've known Jenna for a long time, but we've only recently become close. I'm divorced, too, and have kids of my own. I know how difficult things can get with someone else in the picture and trying to blend families and all the awkwardness that comes with that entire process. You're their father, and I'm not interested in causing any problems."

Jay raised his brows at Dale's forthrightness, and the other man laughed.

"I wanted to get that out of the way so we could all relax," Dale said. "You and Jenna have been divorced for a long time, and she assures me there's nothing else between you." Although it was a statement, the declaration sounded more like a question at the end.

"That's right," Jay confirmed. "There's nothing else between us." He had his eyes focused elsewhere.

Dale visibly relaxed and broke into a full grin. "I hope we can be friends," he said, extending his hand.

Jay shook it heartily. This time, the clamminess was gone. "Absolutely. I want what you want. For us to get along."

They went back inside and Dale sought out Jenna's brother in the living room where a football game played, and Jay continued to the kitchen. He'd say hello, get a snack, and join the men watching the game.

He was about to breach the open door of the kitchen when he heard his ex-mother-in-law say in a fairly loud but angry whisper, "You *have* to tell him."

Metal clanged against metal, like the slam of a lid on a pot. "Mom, this is my decision. Not yours." Jenna's voice vibrated with annoyance.

Jay eased closer, careful not to make a sound.

"You've known for a long time. You should say something."

"Not now."

"When, Jenna? When will be the right time?"

"I don't know!" Jenna hissed. "But it's *not now*. I don't want to spoil the boys' birthday."

Jay felt a little guilty about eavesdropping, but at the same time, he wondered what they were talking about. Could Jenna be ill?

Clearing his throat, he entered the kitchen and the two women almost jumped out of their skin.

"Jay," Martha said, more out of surprise than a greeting. "We didn't know you were here already."

Interesting. If he didn't know better, he'd think that whatever Jenna didn't want to share had something to do with him.

"I've only been here a few minutes. Everything okay?" he asked.

Martha's gaze dropped to the cloth she was wringing in her hand. Jenna crossed her arms and looked everywhere but at him.

"Is everything okay?" Jay asked again. "I couldn't help but overhear—"

Martha's head snapped up.

"What did you overhear?" Jenna asked sharply.

Jay frowned at her. "Not enough to know what's going on."

"There's nothing going on." Jenna turned back to the stove and stirred the meat sauce.

"Excuse me." Martha slid past him out the door.

Jay watched her go and then turned his attention back to his ex, whose rigid stance in front of the stove was an obvious attempt at avoiding conversation.

Something was definitely amiss.

****

When the other kids arrived, the children totaled

ten in all. They crowded into the den to eat and left the adults at the dining table. While they ate, Jay observed Jenna and her mother. Jenna seemed normal, but Martha appeared visibly upset and wouldn't meet his eyes even though she sat right across from him.

Before he left, he had to confront Jenna about what she was keeping from him. He had a right to know if her secret involved the boys. If she was ill, he had a right to know that, too. They needed to prepare themselves and the boys for any outcome.

After dinner, everyone in the house packed into the den and Arturo and Marco opened presents. Jay sat on the floor taking pictures, and Jenna sat in an armchair memorializing the boys' excitement with a video camera.

Their uncle, Ian, eventually wheeled in the scooters Jay had purchased and kept stored at his house. Because Marco was colorblind, his was black and Arturo's was green, his favorite color.

The boys and their friends went into a frenzy for a few minutes. Their excited voices filled the room as they examined the new "toys."

"Cool!"

"Aw man, you're so lucky!"

"Thanks, Dad!"

Jay took a few more photos before he lowered the smartphone and said to Dale. "Would you hand me that red and green wrapped gift right there." He pointed.

Dale sat in one of the armchairs with several presents stacked beside him. The one in question had a big green bow and contained a handmade chess set. The gift was for Arturo, who had developed an avid interest in chess over the past year.

"He can't see those colors, Dad," Marco explained. "He's colorblind, like me."

"Oh really?"

Jenna and her mother froze—Jenna in the chair, her mother seated on its arm. From the corner of his eyes, Jay noted their reaction and how they eyed him.

"That's right, I am," Dale said. He picked up the gift. "But I'm guessing it's this one?" He handed over the box.

Jay might have brushed over the women's reactions if Dale's behavior hadn't undergone a change, too. His easy-going demeanor came off as too easy-going in that moment. *Forced*, would be a better word, and his face reddened. Even Ian watched Jay with an odd expression on his face.

A feeling of unease engulfed him, like an invasion of ants crawling over and under his skin. He suddenly felt as if he was under a microscope, under observation to gauge his reaction. Then a thought hit him.

He stared hard at Dale, still with that affable expression on his face. His head swung in the direction of his ex-wife and her mother. He looked at Marco, now shadowboxing with his brother, and the bottom fell out of his stomach. The sensation intensified when his gaze settled once again on Jenna and Martha.

That's when he knew.

Marco was not his son. Marco was Dale's son.

His heart felt on the verge of exploding.

Everyone knew, but him.

CHAPTER EIGHTEEN

The birthday party had been ruined. At least for the adults.

Jay rested his head on the back of the sofa in the hotel room. Although he didn't want a drink, he *needed* one and ordered a bottle of Scotch from room service. More than anything, he wanted to file away the events of the day and forget them.

Ian and Martha had remained with the kids while Jay, Dale, and Jenna had gone into the kitchen. Jenna had stood sobbing, muttering about how sorry she was and how 'it just happened.'

"I wanted to tell you," Dale had said, but after that, he stared down at the tile and remained silent.

Then Jenna flipped and blamed Jay for the deception.

"It's your fault. You think I don't know that you love her? That you've always loved her?" He didn't even have to ask who she was talking about. "Why do you think I had my father recommend her for the job in Chicago? I had to get her away from you—from us. Something happened the night you took her

home. I shouldn't have allowed it, but it was raining. Something happened, Jay. I know it did. Because afterward you were so different. So I had to do something. I had to."

"So you got pregnant?" He'd suspected, of course, that she'd gotten pregnant on purpose. Yet he couldn't have been happier to be a father.

"I didn't mean to get pregnant by both of you! I came home to get away and yes, I slept with Dale. I was feeling so bad about us and our relationship. I saw the way you looked at her. I saw how she avoided looking at you. I couldn't stand it."

Jay ran trembling fingers through his hair. She'd married him knowing that another man could be the father of her children. Only by chance had paternity been split down the middle. "How long have you known?"

She swiped tears from her cheeks. *"I didn't know right away, I swear. I knew what I'd done, but I hoped the babies were yours. They were twins, for heaven's sake! I only suspected the truth a few months after they were born. Because of the differences."*

That's when she'd no longer allowed him to touch her, when her focus became the boys and he was treated like an outsider in his own home. All along he'd thought it was postpartum symptoms. He'd tried to be understanding, but in reality it had been her own deception keeping them apart.

"I didn't want to think about it," she whispered brokenly. *"I pretended it wasn't true, but when we learned Marco was colorblind, I couldn't avoid the truth anymore. Two years ago we had DNA tests done on both boys, to be sure. Dale is Marco's father."*

A knock on the door signaled his bottle had arrived, and Jay dragged to his feet. The hotel employee smiled broadly, but Jay wasn't in a smiling mood. To make up for his surly attitude, he tipped the young man generously. He couldn't wait to get stinking drunk off the hotel's overpriced liquor.

He sank onto the sofa and placed the bottle and glass on the table in front of him. The room was hazy, like a dream. Unfortunately, this was all real. No matter how much he drank to make the pain of betrayal go away, the truth remained. Jenna had suspected all along. *Suspected,* but never took the steps to confirm paternity. And after she had, she didn't see fit to tell him the truth.

Pain jabbed his chest, as if someone were sticking knives into the cavity.

Jay buried his head in his hands. He'd taught both boys how to swim while on vacation at the family's villa on Lake Maggiore in Turin. He'd taught them how to ride a bike one year when they'd spent the month of July with him in Atlanta.

Those were his boys—both of them. Marco may not have Jay's blood running through his veins, but he was *his* son. Years of betrayal and lies didn't change that.

The yawning ache in his chest widened, and he no longer expected the bottle in front of him could alleviate the pain.

He looked at the phone and wondered....had Brenda known, too? Could she have also been part of the conspiracy to keep the truth from him?

He was about to find out.

****

Brenda snatched up the phone from the bedside table when she heard the special ring tone she'd assigned to Jay's name. She dropped onto the bed, wrapped in a damp towel from the shower she'd taken a few minutes before.

Her heart tripped with trepidation. She sat against

the headboard and drew her feet up on the bed. "How did it go?"

"Did you know about Marco?" Jay asked.

His dead, emotionless voice sounded so completely unlike Jay she was startled and worried at the same time.

"What's going on?"

"Did you know Marco isn't my son?"

Brenda's mouth fell open, the only sound a croak of disbelief before she closed it again. She shook her head in shock. Perhaps she'd misunderstood. "What do you mean he's not your son?"

"Did you know?" he demanded.

"No. Jay, what's going on?"

"Jenna told you everything."

"Not that. I swear to you. My goodness, the boys are...they're *twins*."

He laughed bitterly, and the sound was so anguished she wished she was with him right then so she could hold him. "Fraternal twins. Two different eggs. And in this case, two different fathers."

Brenda couldn't even wrap her mind around the implication of his words. That would mean Jenna had cheated on Jay.

"I swear to you I had no idea. I never even suspected. I assumed Arturo was like your side of the family and Marco took after hers."

"So did I," he said quietly.

"Who's the father?" This was like a bad episode of the "Maury Show."

"Her new boyfriend, Dale. He came to our wedding as a friend, but obviously he had been more than a friend," Jay muttered.

"Jay..." She wanted to reach through the phone

175

and comfort him.

"And she knew you and I had feelings for each other. She didn't urge her father to get you the interview in Chicago because of your friendship. She did it because she wanted to get you away from me."

"What?" Brenda said, her breathing halting. That revelation left her floored.

"I'm here for one more night," Jay said heavily. "I want to spend as much time with my—with my sons as possible."

Brenda held on to the phone tightly, her heart aching for him. "Is there anything I can do? Tell me what you need."

"Nothing."

"You shouldn't be alone."

He huffed out a breath. "I'll be fine."

"Jay…"

"I'll be fine, Brenda. I need time alone to think right now. I'll be in touch."

****

Worry ate at Brenda.

Three days had passed since her conversation with Jay, and she'd tried calling him numerous times, but he hadn't answered his phone. She called Omega Advertising, and his secretary said he'd taken a short leave of absence and wouldn't be back for a few days. Then last night he'd sent a cryptic text asking her to stop trying to contact him. He needed time alone.

He may say he wanted to be left alone, but she was certain that he shouldn't be. She needed to see him, hold him, touch him. Anything to ease his pain and alleviate some of what he must be going through.

She couldn't help him from her apartment, so she packed a bag, hopped in the car, and drove to his house in Alpharetta. It was difficult to drive at a sane pace and not risk injuring herself and other drivers on the road, but she managed.

Upon arrival, she left her bag in the car. She'd been in such a hurry to get to his house, she hadn't grabbed a jacket, and the sheer white blouse and ankle-length skirt she wore were insufficient to keep her comfortable in the cool fall air.

She pressed close to the door of his house and rang the doorbell, rubbing her hands up and down her arms to generate warmth.

She waited.

And waited.

She rang the bell again, certain he was home, but would he leave her out there?

"Open, Jay, please," she whispered. Had she been wrong to come? He'd made it clear he didn't want company, but she'd known him for so long. Knew how much he adored Marco and Arturo. She couldn't let him suffer alone.

She rang the bell one more time, but he still didn't come.

Dejected, Brenda was in a half turn when the door opened.

She'd hoped that when he saw her he would change his mind, but he looked exactly the way he'd sounded on the phone. Solemn, grim. He didn't want her there, but her eyes drank him in. Glorious in a pair of navy blue pajama bottoms, he stared at her with his black hair disheveled, as if she'd disturbed him from sleep.

"I told you I wanted to be alone," he said.

She swallowed. "I know, but I couldn't stay away."

"This is hard for me," he grated.

"I know," she whispered. "Do you want me to go?"

"You shouldn't have come in the first place," he snarled.

If he could say something so hurtful with her standing there, after the times they'd spent together and the moments they'd shared, then she had made a mistake. His rejection humiliated her. What had she been thinking? A few orgasms did not a relationship make.

"Fine," she said, using anger to mask her embarrassment.

But her anger was not directed at him. He was being honest. She was angry at herself for being so brash as to show up unannounced. Obviously he didn't need her.

She swung away but didn't get far. He caught her around the waist and pulled her back against him. He flattened his nose against her neck, the rough hairs on his jaw and chin chafing her skin. The same way they had grated against her inner thighs, her stomach, the tender flesh of her breasts.

She grabbed onto the doorframe for support, already weak-kneed from his touch. The other hand she used to touch his cheek, trembling as he pressed his erection into her bottom. She lifted her hips against him, seeking his heat.

Muttering an oath, he dragged her inside. The door slammed and he pressed her against the door. With her cheek to the wood, he bunched up her skirt and began the climb to her inner thigh.

His hand made contact with the warmth between her legs and gently squeezed. She gasped, having difficulty catching her breath, the need was so great.

It had been less than a week since they last saw each other, but the raw pain of her aching body gave no indication such a short period had passed.

"I need you," he groaned.

Nodding vigorously, she turned in his arms, willing to do anything to ease his anguish. His hands moved under her skirt, and he cupped her bottom as their mouths joined together. He grinded her into the door, prepping her for what was to come. She was ready, soaked, and shaking.

She shoved the pants past his hips, and he peeled off her clothes, one piece at a time. First the skirt, then the thin, practically transparent fabric of her top came off, revealing the swell of her brown breasts over the top of the black demi-cup bra.

She pulled his head down to hers and their tongues lunged toward each other. Naked, skin to skin, the hairs on his chest tickled her nipples and the irregular beat of her heart clamored against his.

His hands went behind her knees and he lifted her and walked toward the carpeted staircase. Instead of climbing to the bedroom, he lowered onto a step and she followed, easing onto his thick shaft. As he entered her body, she moaned and tightened her arms around him. She strained closer, the experience of being filled by him sending a tremble of erotic pleasure coursing through her veins.

Then his lips were on the skin of her neck, at the pulse of her throat, and lower to her aching breasts. Each flick of his tongue was sublime, each suck a pleasure she never wanted to live without. She held on tighter, arching her body, one hand around his neck, the other gripping a baluster on the wooden rail.

They moved in perfect sync, retreating and then

thrusting together in a heated clasp. His hands supported her back as she bounced on top of his pumping hips. Her moans grew louder and her breathing became more sporadic. He pushed his hips with increased fervor, the lean muscles of his stomach contracting with the effort. Their movements became less and less controlled with each passing second, and her hold on him tightened.

They were so in tune with each other that their mutual satisfaction came at the same time. He with a loud shout, and she with a keening cry. Gasping, pumping, they fought through the battering waves of orgasmic bliss. He spilled inside of her, and she shuddered, eyes closed tight, before slumping against him.

They clung to each other on the staircase, their damp bodies loathe to separate. She inhaled deeply, the fragrance of sweat and sex heavy in the air.

Tenderly, gently, she kissed his temple, his cheek, his mouth, and the deep cleft in his chin.

He sighed and buried his face in her neck. "He's my son," he muttered into her skin, his voice thick. "*Mio figlio. Mio figlio.*" *My son. My son.* The hurt emanating from him was almost tangible. It filled his voice, and she felt it in the air.

"I know, honey," she said softly. She stroked her fingers through his fine hair, hugging him close, offering comfort the best way she knew. "I know."

Chapter Nineteen

"Are you okay?" Brenda whispered in the quiet of the room.

She lay wrapped around Jay's back in the immense bed, one leg thrown over his waist, the covers over their hips. The European design of the bedroom furniture was evident in the clean lines of the two large dressers and the matching stands on either side of the bed.

She ran a hand up and down his muscular arm which lay lightly on her thigh, keeping her close to him. "Do you want to talk?" she asked quietly.

He didn't answer right away, and she continued to caress his arm in a soothing motion. Over the smooth, corded muscles and down to the strength of his hair sprinkled forearms. Back and forth, back and forth.

"No," he said finally. "But I feel better having you here. I feel as if I can finally face this thing."

She kissed his back. "You can, and we'll figure it out."

She wondered when he and Jenna planned to tell Marco and Arturo. And would Dale want to take on a more active role in his son's life now that the secret was out? Would he stop Jay from moving Marco to Atlanta to live?

A loud pounding came from downstairs, jarring her from her thoughts.

Jay groaned. "Who the hell is that at this hour?" he mumbled. He reached for the phone on the nightstand and checked the time.

The mystery person was pounding very loud and hadn't taken a break. Immediately after that thought, the steady beating stopped and was followed by the chime of the doorbell.

Who in the world...?

"Stay here," Jay said.

She had no intention of moving from the warm and comfy bed. She burrowed deeper under the blankets, rolling over into the warmth and scent left behind by Jay's body.

She watched him tug on his pajama bottoms and walk out of the bedroom.

The pounding started again and Brenda frowned. Who could be so rude?

Jay had left the bedroom door ajar, and she strained her ear to hear the uninvited guest. The sound of a loud male voice traveled up to the second floor and into the room. She cocked her head and listened closely.

That sounded like Nick!

Brenda scrambled from the bed and grabbed Jay's terry cloth robe from the bathroom door. It swallowed her, so large it fell around her ankles and almost wrapped around her twice. She tiptoed into the hall and peered down into the foyer, careful not to be seen.

"I know she's here," Nick said. She saw the top of his head. Unleashed anger filled his voice.

"You shouldn't have come here," Jay told him in a calm voice.

"Tell me she's not here, and I'll leave. Tell me that's not her car outside."

"She's not here."

"You're a liar!" Nick made a menacing move toward Jay, and Brenda held her breath.

Jay didn't cower. "Get out of my house. You're acting like a maniac."

Nick stuck a finger in Jay's face. "You're a backstabber, and you're no friend of mine."

Jay continued to stare at him calmly, but the muscles of his back and shoulders were rigid with tension. "You have a couple of options. Leave now, peacefully, or I'll toss you out."

Nick didn't budge. His hand closed into a fist at his side, and his chest heaved up and down as he pulled in lungful after lungful of air. He looked ready to charge, then thought better of it and swung back to the door.

Jay followed, but at the last minute, Nick swung around and landed a fist straight to his temple.

The wild punch knocked Jay backward into the entryway table. He reached out to hold on, but the furniture was no match for his weight. Jay, the table, and a vase crashed to the floor. The vase shattered and pieces of glass launched in a dozen directions.

"Jay!" Brenda screamed. She rushed down the stairs.

Nick looked up, the fury in his face changing into

surprise, and then morphing into fury again. "I knew you'd lied to me!" he yelled at Jay, taking a step toward him.

Jay came to his feet, shaking his head from the dizzying effect of the sucker punch.

Brenda placed her body between them, careful to avoid the chunks of glass on the floor. She lifted one hand to Jay's bare chest and the other in the air toward Nick. "Stop it! You have no right to question who I'm with or where I am."

"How could you sleep with him?" Nick demanded. Wild, angry eyes shot accusations at her. "You slept with me!"

"We didn't mean for this to happen. It wasn't planned."

"You expect me to believe you didn't plan this?" He looked from one to the other. "What, were the two of you screwing all this time? While he was married to Jenna?"

"It's none of your damn business," Jay said, rubbing his temple. He glowered at Nick.

"No," Brenda answered. Jay may not care, but she wanted to de-escalate the tense situation. "Nothing happened between us while he was married and we only recently started seeing each other."

"We don't owe him an explanation," Jay growled behind her.

"Do you really think I want to hear this shit?" Nick asked her, his face contorted into an angry, disgusted mask. His gaze panned to Jay. "I told you how I felt about her, and you stabbed me in the fucking back. You bastard."

Brenda attempted to bring his attention back to her. "This wasn't planned, Nick. We didn't mean to—

"

"And you lied when I asked you two seconds ago whether or not she was here."

"You showed up at my house angry and yelling. I did what any rational person would do—try to avoid a confrontation, you asshole."

"I'm an asshole?" Nick jabbed his finger at Jay. "*You* were supposed to keep tabs on her."

"I never agreed to your idiotic idea."

"Now I know why!"

"Nick." Brenda stepped directly in front of Nick's line of vision. She kept her voice low and conciliatory. "We didn't set out to hurt you. Believe me, we were worried about how our relationship would affect the friendship between all of us."

It seemed Nick didn't even hear her words. His mottled face was still an intimidating mask of deep emotion. The fists clenched at his side indicated his strong desire to rage and hit Jay again.

"I came down here on business and on the way to the hotel, Jenna called me crying and told me everything about Marco. Said she needed a friend. A real one, because you and Brenda were together now, but I didn't want to believe it. I came over here to confront you, and then I saw Brenda's car." He shook his head, pumped up by hurt and anger. "She was right about the two of you. Her so-called friend is sneaking around with her ex-husband."

The words stung. They sounded dirty and sordid.

"I couldn't care less what you think about us," Jay said. "It doesn't change anything between me and Brenda."

"Do the two of you think you're in love or something?" Nick sneered.

There was a moment of silence before Jay's voice came from behind her. "Yes, I'm in love with her."

Brenda's heart took an enormous leap. She veered in Jay's direction. They hadn't discussed their feelings in depth. She knew how she felt about him, but hearing him verbalize his feelings was not only a relief, she gained the confidence she needed.

"I'm in love with him, too," she said quietly, looking into his eyes.

Jay smiled softly at her.

"Do I need to leave so the two of you can have your moment?" Nick growled.

Brenda reluctantly wrenched her eyes away from Jay and back to her friend. "We can't help how we feel about each other."

"What about me?" he asked.

"There was never anything between us, Nick. You know that."

"You never felt *anything* after that night in Italy?" The pleading in his eyes and voice made her sad. He still cared so deeply for her.

"I never had those kinds of feelings for you," she said softly, and the hurt in his eyes was almost unbearable.

Nick stared at the floor. "I wanted to give you the world," he said thickly.

"I don't want the world," she said. "Nick." His head popped up, and the sheen of tears in his eyes hurt her even more, expanding the pain in her chest. But she couldn't do this halfway. She had to be clear so he didn't hold onto false hope. "You should have someone in your life who can love you the way you want to be loved."

His jaw tightened. "That someone should be you."

"No." Brenda shook her head, arms folded over her chest. She didn't want him to have the burden of that thought. She'd found love and so would he.

He backed toward the door. His withdrawal hurt because it meant the friendship had come to an end, for all three of them.

Nick's eyes remained on her for a while, as if engraving her image in his mind. His gaze swept the tousled hair, which must be sticking up in all directions on her head, glaring evidence of the intimacy she and Jay had shared. His eyes drifted over Jay's oversized robe and continued on down to her bare feet.

Then he looked past her to Jay. His mouth became a flat line and his eyes hardened in a surge of anger. One more time he gave her his attention, and then nodded, as if finally understanding that he truly didn't stand a chance.

Without another word, he turned around and slammed the door on his way out.

Arms still wrapped tight around her torso, Brenda turned slowly to face Jay. He stood with his arms hanging loosely at his sides, worry etched in the lines of his forehead. An unsightly red knot protruded from his left temple.

"Your face," Brenda said. The heaviness in her heart made her voice tremble.

"I'm fine." He lifted a hand to her. "Come here."

She stepped over a piece of glass and into his arms.

"Soon, you won't hurt so much. Okay?" Jay said.

She nodded against his chest and held on tight. Tears blurred her vision, and even though she hurt, she trusted his words and believed in them as a couple.

"Okay."

CHAPTER TWENTY

Marco and Arturo came charging through the swinging door of the kitchen.

"Boys!" Brenda said sharply. She shot them a stern look. "You know better."

They skidded to a halt.

"Sorry, Brenda," Arturo said.

Christmas carols filled the air, and the scent of gingerbread and mulled cider permeated the entire downstairs. Brenda was in the midst of prepping for when the rest of the guests arrived. Sophie was on her way, coming alone. Thanks to a conversation she'd had with Jay, Keith was permanently out of her life and she was on a break from dating.

A couple of the interns from the magazine were also coming over. Brenda had invited them so they wouldn't have to spend the holiday alone.

Jay's father and his girlfriend had flown in a few days ago and were staying at the house, while Brenda's mother and her fiancé had chosen to get a room at a nearby hotel.

"What are you two doing in here, anyway?" Brenda asked. She opened the package of cinnamon sticks and proceeded to place one in each of the glass mugs. The fragrant spice would serve as a garnish for the cider.

"We're bored," Marco said.

"With all those gifts?" Jay had spoiled the boys rotten with video games, clothes, and remote-controlled planes and cars. She shook her head. "In my day…"

The boys groaned and rolled their eyes.

Brenda chuckled. "Okay, okay, never mind. How about helping me out while you're here? Take those cookies, those nuts, and the cannoli to the dining room and set them on the sidebar."

"You're putting us to work." Marco pouted.

"You said you were bored, so I'm giving you something to do."

"You and your big mouth," Arturo said in a stage whisper.

Brenda hid her smile. Having them around had brightened the holiday. She and Jay had decorated with a wreath on the door and blinking lights on the windows, but they'd saved the tree trimming until the boys arrived. The four of them had decorated the tree together, although Jay had left it mostly to them while he videotaped. Afterward, they'd watched "A Christmas Story" with large mugs of hot cocoa containing mini marshmallows.

The boys were going to stay the entire two weeks they were off from school. She and Jay had lots of activities planned, including a trip to go ice skating, which should be interesting since neither she nor he knew how to skate.

The doorbell rang.

"That's probably Sophie," Marco said in a hushed voice. His eyes lit up. He had a crush on her friend. He dashed out empty-handed.

Arturo shook his head and took the tray of cookies in hand. "Kids," he said.

Brenda burst out laughing. He was only ten minutes older than his brother, but he liked poking fun at Marco.

After Arturo left, Brenda's mother, Samantha, came into the kitchen. "Need some help, baby?"

As part of the day's festivities, everyone had to wear an ugly sweater. Her mother had gone against the grain in a pair of jeans—the loosest fit Brenda had ever seen her wear—and an olive-brown cowl-neck sweater. Her understated appearance had shocked Brenda, but she figured the change in style probably had a lot to do with Basil's influence.

"I'm fine. You doing okay?" She poured hot cider into the glass mugs.

"Fine."

She knew her mother had more to say, and she quietly filled each cup and waited.

"He's not exactly what I expected." There it was.

"No, he's not," Brenda agreed.

"You could have told me he was white."

"Does it matter?" Brenda continued filling the glasses.

Her mother shrugged. "It would have been nice to know ahead of time. I'm sure he thought I was rude for staring."

"Not really. I'm not exactly what his father expected, either. We purposely didn't tell either of you so you and Gino wouldn't arrive with any preconceived notions."

"*You're* wonderful. Gino would be lucky to have you as a daughter-in-law." Her mother sniffed.

Brenda poured cider into the last mug and set the pitcher on the counter. "Thank you, Sam. Jay's a great guy, too. I hope you give him a chance."

"I'm sure he's a wonderful man, but what's going to happen when the two of you have kids? They're going to have an identity crisis. Are they black, are they white? Should they be called biracial? You have to think about these things."

Brenda placed a hand on her hip. "You're getting ahead of yourself. Let me and Jay worry about that. Any other concerns?"

Her mother shrugged, drawing circles in the speckled pattern of the counter. "He has to be good to you. I care about that." She cast a sidelong glance at Brenda. "He *is* good to you, isn't he?"

"Yes, he is."

Samantha brushed the front of her sweater, even though there was nothing to brush. "Because I guess that's the most important thing—that he's good to you, and you're happy."

Brenda took her mother's hand in hers. "I'm very happy. And I'm happy for you. I like Basil."

Her mother's eyes filled with relief. "Do you? He's a wonderful man. Can you tell?"

"Yes, I can tell."

During the short period she'd seen them together, she recognized Basil was the kind of man her mother had needed all her life. Someone to show her love and respect, but also someone who wouldn't tolerate her outrageous behavior. He opened doors and held her hand, and smiled at her with such fondness in his eyes, no one could doubt he genuinely cared for her.

She squeezed her mother's hand. "You did good, Sam."

"I did, didn't I?" Tears filled her eyes. "I did good this time."

"Yeah, you did." They hugged each other, and at that moment Brenda realized how much her mother had longed for the approval of others. Even from her own daughter.

Samantha pulled back and fanned her face. "You're gonna make me cry." She sniffed. "I wish your sister could have been here."

Tracey had declined the invitation to come for Christmas when she found out Samantha would be there. Brenda hadn't divulged that tidbit, but no doubt her mother had guessed the reason for Tracey's absence. "I'll talk to her for you."

"Okay." Samantha patted her cheek. "You're such a good daughter, you know that? I don't know how I lucked out and had such a good kid." She rubbed her hands together. "Okay, what do you need me to get for you?"

"Can you grab those nuts and place them on the sideboard? I'll be out in a few minutes."

"Not a problem. Basil loves nuts." She picked up the three-compartment tray with Brazil nuts, peanuts, and cashews and exited the kitchen, almost colliding with Jay.

"Whoa," he said, placing a steadying hand on her arms.

They both laughed and he held the door open so she could slide out.

"Maybe you should remove that door," Brenda said. "It's kind of dangerous. What do you think?"

Jay came to stand beside her. He'd truly gotten into the spirit of the ugly sweater game. His was a hideous thing with every possible seasonal item on it in a breathtakingly hideous collage—Santa, holly, a Christmas tree, Rudolph, a snowman, snowflakes— and that was only the front. He still looked just as sexy as ever, though. Not even that dreadful piece of clothing could detract from his broad shoulders and manly form.

"I think I'm going to strangle my father today," he muttered.

"You're not going to strangle your father. Have a cannolo." Sweet Treats Bakery had rolled out Christmas cannoli, decorated with red and green candied fruit and dusted with powdered sugar. "Tell me what happened."

"He had the nerve to say that if he were still running the business, it would be farther along right now. Our company has grown by leaps and bounds since I took over, but will he give me credit? Of course not." He cursed in Italian, something he'd been doing a lot of since his father arrived.

Brenda handed him a cannolo. He took the pastry and bit into it. As he chewed, the tension in his shoulders decreased.

"He's only here for a couple more days," she reminded him.

Jay laughed a little to himself. "See what he does to me?"

"No different than my mother," Brenda said. "But she's been good, so I can't complain too much."

"Well, I can get through anything as long as you're by my side," Jay said.

That statement would be put to the test very soon.

He and Dale had not been able to come to terms regarding Marco, and a court date had been set for the beginning of the year. Dale wanted full parental rights and didn't want Marco moving to Atlanta. Jay was fine with Dale getting involved in his biological son's life, but he rejected the idea of splitting up the boys.

Brenda rose on the tip of her shoes and gave Jay a soft kiss, savoring the taste of chocolate and pistachio from the dessert he'd eaten.

"Behave yourself," he said, smiling against her mouth.

"I can't when I'm around you."

She pinched his bottom, and he grabbed her around the waist. Brenda squealed when he backed her into the refrigerator.

"You sure you want to play this game?" he asked.

"Someone could come in here," she whispered.

"So what? All they would see is a man kissing his future wife."

"Mmm…future wife. I like the sound of that." She looped an arm around his neck.

They planned to get married in the late spring, hopefully after the situation with Marco was resolved. They didn't want to put it off too long. They'd waited long enough, and Charlie's sudden death earlier this year had shown them the importance of seizing the moment. They wanted to be man and wife as soon as possible.

They kissed again, more deeply this time. His mouth covered hers with soft, moist kisses that made her groan with regret when they pulled apart.

Jay sighed. "We have a house full of guests."

"Yes, we do." Brenda sighed, too.

She picked up the tray of cups filled with cider and Jay grabbed the tray of cannoli. He walked over to the kitchen door and held it open for her. They both took a deep breath and pasted on smiles. As she walked by him, Jay whispered, "I love you."

Her eyes met his, and a smile softened her features. "Love you, too."

They walked out to face their families.

Together.

The End

More Stories by
Delaney Diamond

Hot Latin Men series
The Arrangement
Fight for Love
Private Acts
Second Chances
Hot Latin Men: Vol. I (print anthology)
Hot Latin Men: Vol. II (print anthology)

Hawthorne Family series
The Temptation of a Good Man
A Hard Man to Love
Here Comes Trouble
For Better or Worse
Hawthorne Family Series: Vol. I (print anthology)
Hawthorne Family Series: Vol. II (print anthology)

Love Unexpected series
The Blind Date
The Wrong Man
An Unexpected Attraction
The Right Time (coming soon)

Johnson Family series
Unforgettable
Perfect
Just Friends (spring 2015)
The Rules (coming soon)

Bailar series (sweet/clean romance)
Worth Waiting For

Short Stories
Subordinate Position
The Ultimate Merger

Free Stories
http://DelaneyDiamond.com

ABOUT THE AUTHOR

Delaney Diamond is the USA Today Bestselling Author of sweet, sensual, passionate romance novels. Originally from the U.S. Virgin Islands, she now lives in Atlanta, Georgia. She reads romance novels, mysteries, thrillers, and a fair amount of nonfiction. When she's not busy reading or writing, she's in the kitchen trying out new recipes, dining at one of her favorite restaurants, or traveling to an interesting locale. She speaks fluent conversational French and can get by in Spanish.

Enjoy free reads and the first chapter of all her novels on her website. Join her e-mail mailing list to get sneak peeks, notices of sale prices, and find out about new releases.

http://DelaneyDiamond.com